What Teachers and Students are saying about the

MANITOU ART CAPER

Miss LuValley

More of What People are Saying

"Manitou Art Caper is a book that children and adults alike will love! The plot is suspenseful, and every chapter leaves the reader compelled to continue. As a third grade teacher, I am always looking for good books to add to my library. However, more importantly, I am looking for books that will be of interest to my students from the very beginning and keep them interested throughout the book. Manitou Art Caper definitely does that. I will recommend this book to my students for many years to come!"

Betsy Sterling
Third Grade Teacher
Cherry Creek School District

"This book was easy to follow and fun to read."

Evan – 10

"I liked the book because it got me thinking and the characters made it fun."

Kirsten - 10

"I thoroughly enjoyed reading Manitou Art Caper. It is wonderfully written with vivid imagery and the mystery element keeps you completely drawn into the book and its characters."

Sue
Director of Children's Ministries

"Manitou Art Caper is a book full of suspense and mystery. The plot was very interesting."

Rasesh - 10

Rocky Mountain Mysteries™

MANITOU ART CAPER

Emily Burns

Illustrated By
John Breeding

Covered Wagon Publishing LLC

ROCKY MOUNTAIN MYSTERIES: 2
    MANITOU ART CAPER

Copyright © 2002 by Covered Wagon Publishing, LLC. All Rights Reserved.
No part of this publication may be reproduced, stored in a retrieval system, or transmitted, in any form or by any means, electronic, mechanical, photocopying, or otherwise, without the prior written permission of Covered Wagon Publishing, LLC. The information in this book is furnished for informational use only, and is subject to change without notice. Covered Wagon Publishing, LLC assumes no responsibility for any errors or inaccuracies that may appear in this book.

All images, logos and trademarks included in this book are subject to use according to trademark and copyright laws of the United States of America. Trivial Pursuit Junior is a trademark of Horn Abbott Ltd. and distributed by Hasbro Inc.. Rocky Mountain Mysteries is a trademark of Covered Wagon Publishing LLC

ISBN: 0-9723259-1-3

10 9 8 7 6 5 4 3 2 First Printing: January 2003

Printed in the United States of America by:
    KNI, Incorporated
    1261 South College Parkway • Anaheim, CA 92806
    Cover printed on 10PT C1S- Bright white cover with lay-flat gloss laminate.
    Interior pages printed on 60# White Smooth Offset

Published and distributed by

                            Covered Wagon Publishing, LLC,
                            PO Box 473038 Aurora, Colorado 80047-3038.
                            jackd@coveredwagonpublishing.com

Library of Congress Control Number: 2002113538

Illustrated by John Breeding

Book Design, Cover Design and Art Direction by

    A. J. Images Inc.
    Communication & Graphic Design
    www.ajimagesinc.com – 303•696•9227

For educational and individual sales information,
call Covered Wagon Publishing, 1.303.751.0992
Visit our web site at: http://www.RockyMountainMysteries.com

Acknowledgements

We would like to thank all of the businesses
that allowed us to include their names in this book.
These include: Briarhurst Manor, Manitou Jack's,
Miramont Castle, Michael Garman's Studio,
Casa Bonita, and Cheyenne Mountain Zoo.

Thanks also goes out to
all the teachers, parents, and kids
who have contributed
to the success of this series.

Dedicated to my mother and my brother, Roger,
both of whom I admire more than they will ever know.
I thank my mother for her guidance,
understanding, and unconditional love.
I thank my brother for always being there for me
and for not only being a wonderful brother,
but also a good friend.

Tyler -

is sixteen years old and has brown hair and brown eyes. His hobbies include camping, fishing, baseball, and white water rafting. His best friend is Dylan.

Dylan -

is sixteen years old with reddish/brown hair. He is on the high school football team and enjoys fishing, watching movies, and hanging out with his friends.

Stephanie -

is fourteen years old and a twin to her brother, Steve. She enjoys reading, writing, and playing the piano. Stephanie's best friend is Kamryn.

Kamryn -

is thirteen years old with blond hair and blue eyes. Her hobbies include shopping, music, reading, the drama club, playing games, and bike riding.

Steve -

has light brown hair and hazel eyes like his twin sister. His favorite pastime is baseball. He enjoys reading, camping, photography, and fishing. His best friend is Andrew.

Andrew -

is thirteen years old with brown hair and brown eyes. His hobbies include wrestling, baseball, swimming, and collecting trading cards.

Contents

Chapter 1
Hot Pursuit

"Rash of Art Robberies Puzzle Police." Marybeth Thompson showed her brother, Jack, and his family the headline on the front page of the *Gazette Telegraph*.

The family had just arrived at Marybeth's art gallery, the Fountain Gallery, in Manitou Springs.

Jack and his wife, Carol, professional travel writers, were going on a trip to Albuquerque and Santa Fe, New Mexico, to write an article on the area. Tyler, Steve, and Stephanie, whose summer vacation had just started, were staying with their Aunt Marybeth while their parents were away.

Concerned about his sister's art gallery, Jack Thompson read the article that his sister had shown him while the family greeted each other.

Fourteen-year-old Stephanie, who had light brown hair with hazel eyes, as does her twin brother, Steve, was the first to hug her aunt.

"What about you boys?" their aunt asked. "Tyler, just because you're old enough to drive doesn't mean you're too old to give your aunt a hug and kiss, does it?"

"It doesn't sound like the police have any leads yet," Jack commented when he had finished reading the article.

"No, it sure doesn't, and it looks like I won't have much time to spend with you kids during your visit," she sighed. "I think I had better stay close to my store and watch for anything peculiar."

"That's ok, we'll still have fun," brown-haired Tyler said as he and Steve gave their aunt a hug and a kiss.

The teenagers had visited their aunt on several occasions. She always took the kids around to the many galleries in the area, which soon became boring. They were glad to hear that they would get to spend more time on their own during this visit.

"Gee, Marybeth, if it's too much to leave the kids with you . . ." Carol Thompson started to say.

"Nonsense, I have been looking forward to this visit," Aunt Marybeth said. "Besides, they will want to see their cousin, Alex."

"Alex is coming?" fourteen-year-old Steve asked when he heard his cousin's name.

"Yes, Uncle Matt and Aunt Lisa have decided to take a short vacation to the Caribbean. We're picking Alex up at the airport tomorrow night," Aunt Marybeth said.

The Thompson kids were excited to hear that they would get to see their cousin, who was just a year younger than Tyler. Uncle Matt was an Emergency Medical Technician and his career had led the family to Southern California where his job was very hectic and stressful. It wasn't often that the teenagers had the chance to see their cousin.

"Maybe we should call off the big camping trip that the kids have planned," Carol said referring to a campout that they had planned months before with their best friends.

"No, I don't think there is any reason to do that," Aunt Marybeth said. "Besides, I know how excited they are to use the new tent they won at the end of the school year."

"We collected a lot of books to get that tent," Steve said.

"The kids are old enough to take care of themselves," Jack Thompson reassured his wife and then asked his sister if she would have lunch with them.

"Sure, I've already arranged for my associate, June, to watch the gallery," she answered.

The family drove down the street to a well-known restaurant in the area, the Briarhurst Manor.

After they had been seated, Tyler asked his aunt how long the robberies had been going on.

"It started about three months ago in Colorado Springs. The thieves hit one of the smaller art galleries downtown and stole a whole collection of art by a local artist named Bruce Duncan. Then, about a week later another shop on the city's west side was broken into and again it was only Bruce Duncan's work that was taken. Since then, several galleries in downtown Manitou Springs have been broken into," Aunt Marybeth told them.

"Maybe we can solve this mystery *too*," Steve said.

"What do you mean too?" their Aunt asked.

"We just solved a mystery about a haunted library and a hidden key," Stephanie said.

"It sounds like you kids have been very busy," their Aunt said as the kids went into more detail about their first adventure, <u>Mystery on Rampart Hill.</u>

"Yeah, and now we have a chance to solve another mystery," Steve said. "Maybe we could sleep in your back room and catch this thief if he breaks into your gallery."

"I don't think so! That would be much too dangerous," Aunt Marybeth exclaimed.

"Sis, maybe you should hire a security guard," Jack suggested.

"That may be a good idea," she said after thinking about it for a few minutes. "I'm sure that the thieves are long gone from this area but why take chances."

Everyone enjoyed lunch at the Briarhurst Manor, and soon they were ready for dessert. While the adults each had a slice of pie, the teenagers enjoyed hot fudge sundaes.

"Boy, you kids sure have an appetite today," their father commented.

"We need lots of energy for our vacation and our camping trip. I can't wait till Kamryn comes so we can go camping," Stephanie said, referring to her best friend.

"We still have to decide where we are going to camp," said Steve, who was just as excited as his sister. The teenagers had narrowed down a list of half a dozen campgrounds with their friends before they left, but they wanted to visit the campgrounds before picking a specific one.

"We'll go check out the campgrounds before the others get here," Tyler said.

The family finished lunch and headed back to the gallery. The teenagers moved their bags into their aunt's car and said good-bye to their parents.

"You have our numbers if you need us," Carol Thompson told her kids.

"Don't worry about us, Mom," Tyler said.

On the way back to Aunt Marybeth's house, their aunt told them that they could use her truck while they visited.

"It's a little banged up, but it'll get you where you want to go," she said.

"Thanks for letting us use it," Tyler said. "We'll take good care of it."

Aunt Marybeth lived in a large Victorian house that sat on the top of a small hill looking down into Manitou Springs. The house was painted a pale yellow with lavender shutters and trim, making it look like a little gingerbread house. The outside of the house was very deceiving as it made the house look small when it was really very large.

On the left side of the foyer, there was a room that was used only for displaying antiques. It had once been a parlor and had French doors that closed it off. Stephanie, who was interested in antiques, liked going into the room to see if her aunt had added anything new to her collection of Victorian furniture.

The living room was similar to the antique room in that it was hardly used but was more for decoration. In the room, there was an antique sofa and love seat but the pieces were not as valuable as the ones in the antique room. There was also a player piano that the teenagers liked to listen to.

The family room was more relaxed, with bookcases on both sides of a large stone fireplace, easy chairs, wrap-around sofa, big screen television, and surround-sound stereo system. The kids often hung out in this room.

Upstairs there were five bedrooms and a full attic that the kids liked to explore. Whenever they visited, they each had their own bedroom just like they had at home. They found their bedrooms and unpacked their suitcases into the drawers that Aunt Marybeth had left ready for them.

When they were done unpacking, they decided to go back downtown to hang out until Aunt Marybeth closed up her art gallery. No matter how often they visited Manitou Springs, they always enjoyed going into the unique gift shops that lined the main street.

The three of them went into Manitou Jack's, one of their favorite shops. The store was known for its large collection of gold jewelry, pottery, and sand paintings. The kids picked out some T-shirts and, after paying for them, headed down the street.

After going into a few more shops they remembered the arcade. Last summer they came upon it the day before they had left. It had all kinds of video games and was a hangout for many teens in the area. It didn't take long for each of them to find a video game to play.

They were having so much fun; they didn't realize what time it was.

"We had better get back to Aunt Marybeth's store," Tyler told his brother and sister.

They were headed down the street toward Aunt Marybeth's gallery when Stephanie stopped them.

"Hey, guys," she called to her brothers. "I want to go into this shop. It's really cool."

"Only for a minute," her older brother Tyler replied. "It's getting late."

The three of them entered the shop, which contained valuable collections and lots of antiques. Stephanie was admiring an antique vase when she and her brothers overhead a customer in the store asking, "Do you have anything done by Bruce Duncan?"

"Bruce Duncan!" Tyler whispered to his sister and brother. "That's the artist whose paintings have been stolen!"

"I am sorry, we do not," answered the owner. "Bruce Duncan has sure become popular lately. Thomas Richly has done work similar to his..."

"I wouldn't be interested," the man answered hastily as he left the shop.

"Let's follow him," Steve suggested.

Stephanie quickly agreed but their older brother thought it might be too suspicious for all three of them to follow.

Reluctantly, Steve and Stephanie stayed behind while Tyler started to follow the man. The man had dark brown hair and looked to be around forty-years-old. A few blocks down the street near a fountain, the man met two other men who appeared to be around the same age.

Tyler stayed as far back as he could, straining to hear their conversation.

"I didn't have any luck," the man told the other two.

"I didn't have any luck either," one of the men, who had brown hair with a reddish tint, replied.

"Tomorrow, we will just have to try some more shops. We will meet again at the same time near the fountain," the first man said.

Tyler started to turn away before the men noticed him but he was too late.

"Hey, you, kid! What do you think you are doing?" one of the men yelled as they spotted Tyler.

Tyler started sprinting down the street with the three men after him in hot pursuit!

Chapter 2
Suspicious Activity

Luckily, Tyler was a fast runner and he had gotten a good head start. When he was about three blocks ahead of the men, he turned down a side alley. He doubted that they saw him but he didn't want to take any chances so he ran a couple more blocks to a park where he slipped into a public restroom. He waited inside holding his breath and peeking out the window. After waiting about a half an hour, he cautiously stepped outside the building.

He didn't see the men anywhere so he went back to the shop where he had left his sister and brother. When he walked in the door, still out of breath, the two rushed over to him.

"We were getting worried!" Stephanie said.

"Yeah, what took so long?" Steve asked.

"Three men were chasing me, and I had to lose them. Then, I had to make sure they had given up looking for me," he started to explain.

"Chasing you?" the shop clerk exclaimed, coming over to where he was standing. "Whatever for, what did you do?"

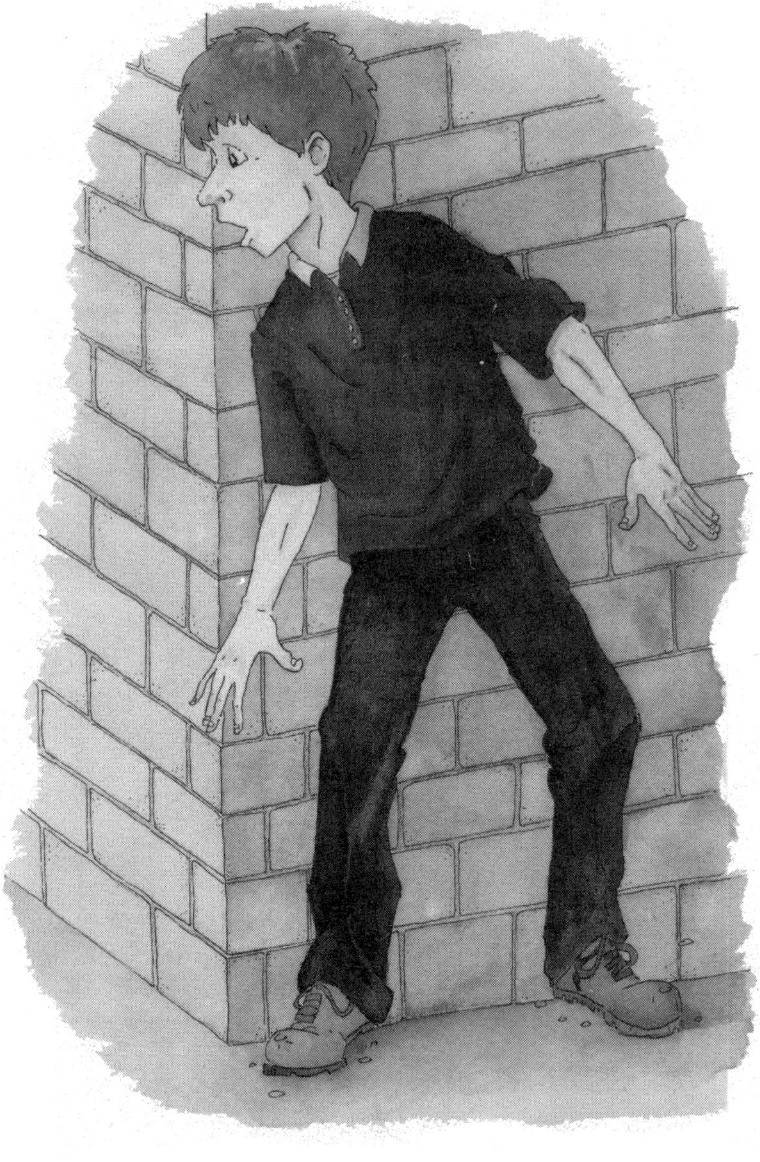

Tyler started at the beginning and explained to her what had happened.

"Those men must be up to something or else they wouldn't have chased you," she reasoned. "We better file a police report."

"We better call Aunt Marybeth also," Stephanie said. "She will be getting worried."

After the shop clerk called the police, Stephanie called her aunt and gave her a brief account of what had happened and told her not to worry.

"We'll come down to your shop as soon as we give our report to the police," she told her aunt.

"Oh no, stay right there. I'll be right over; those men may still be in the area," she replied.

Aunt Marybeth arrived just as the police were pulling up in their car.

"Thank God you kids are all right," she said, hugging each of them.

Tyler tried not to leave any details out as he told the police what had happened.

One of the officers stated that he could not arrest the men because no actual crime had been committed.

"If you remember anything you forgot to tell me, just call me at the station," he said.

That night at dinner the teenagers got their aunt's permission to go up to her attic. It was one of the activities that they always enjoyed doing at her house, ever since they had helped their aunt move in. They had found several boxes in the attic that the previous owners had left behind and had a lot of fun going through them. Since then, not a visit had ever gone by without the teens exploring the attic. Aunt Marybeth quickly gave her permission. She had a special surprise in the attic for them this time.

Just as they were finishing dinner, the teens' parents called to say they had made it to Albuquerque.

"Everyone is fine here," Marybeth told her brother, not mentioning the events that had taken place earlier that afternoon. After the twins talked to their parents, they rushed up to the attic while Tyler sat at the kitchen table with a blank look on his face.

"Aren't you going to join your brother and sister?" his aunt asked him.

"No, I don't feel like exploring at the moment," he said. "Do you have more newspaper clippings on the robberies?"

"Yes, I think so," she said, and then frowned. "Tyler, I don't want you getting mixed up in these robberies. It is much too dangerous."

"There's no harm in letting me read the articles," he said.

His aunt gave in and handed Tyler the newspapers. Tyler read the articles, not knowing what to look for. The men who had chased him just had to be connected to the robberies. They must have been looking for more Bruce Duncan paintings to steal. But as Tyler read article after article in the papers, he questioned if the men were even involved. The articles all said that only one person was ever seen leaving the scene. He also learned another fact that was very interesting: Bruce Duncan had recently passed away.

"It says here that Bruce Duncan appeared to have suffered a heart attack, but that hasn't been confirmed yet," Tyler said.

"Apparently, the doctors ran some tests, which all pointed to a heart attack," Aunt Marybeth told Tyler. "Everyone who knew him was surprised since the man appeared to be fit as a fiddle."

"It could have been foul play for insurance money," Tyler said.

"I guess anything is possible," Aunt Marybeth said, shrugging her shoulders.

Tyler went up to the attic to tell his brother and sister about what he had learned.

"Maybe only one of the three men that you followed, did the actual robbery," Steve suggested.

"That could be," Tyler agreed.

"Tyler, look what we found," Stephanie said holding up a map. "It's a really old map of Colorado."

"I don't remember ever seeing that," Tyler said.

"There is a lot of stuff up here that I've never seen before," Stephanie stated, showing them a small pile of boxes.

As the three of them looked through the boxes, they found Manitou Springs souvenirs, Indian trinkets, and a box of books.

"Hey, here are some books by one of my favorite authors, Alice Chadwick," Stephanie said.

"Look, Tyler, here is a whole box of fishing gear," Steve told his brother.

Tyler looked through the box. Everything in the box was brand new.

"Guys, these boxes don't just happen to be here," he told them. "I think Aunt Marybeth put these things here for us."

Just as he said that, Aunt Marybeth was coming up the attic stairs.

"I see you found your presents," she said, smiling.

The twins were the first ones to hug their aunt, with Tyler right behind them.

"Aunt Marybeth, you shouldn't have," Tyler said.

"I can spoil my niece and nephews if I want to," she said. "Just remember, there is plenty to do without you getting involved in any mysteries."

The next day the teenagers decided to check out some of the campgrounds before going to Denver to pick up their cousin, Alex.

The first campground was a few miles outside of Woodland Park on Lake Manitou. It was a small campground and seemed very quiet but it didn't have everything that they were looking for.

Only a few miles north of Lake Manitou, there was a campground on Rampart Reservoir, a much larger lake. It was a good place to go fishing and allowed small boats, but there wasn't much else.

The next camping area that they went to was located near Mueller State Park. It had everything that they were looking for, such as swimming, fishing, horseback riding, and activities every night.

"This campground has a lot to offer but it seems like it's mainly for RV's," Stephanie said, and her brothers quickly agreed.

"I guess we are spoiled by all the campgrounds near where we live," Tyler commented.

They stopped for lunch at a Chinese restaurant on the edge of town. They discussed the campground possibilities. They wanted to go someplace that was new and adventurous.

"I would really like to find a place that has white water rafting," Tyler said as he looked through a camping guide.

"We want a place that has bike rentals," Steve said.

"You can ride bikes anywhere," Tyler said.

"Yeah, and you can go white water rafting at home," Steve said.

"I'm sure we can find a campground that we can all agree on. We just have to find one that has something for everyone," Stephanie said so her brothers would not start a big argument.

Her brothers nodded in agreement as the waiter served their food. Tyler ordered Pepper Steak, Steve had Chinese Chicken, and Stephanie had her favorite, Sweet and Sour Pork. By the time they had finished eating, they had picked out one more campground to look at.

"Let's head out to Indian Head Campground while we still have time," Tyler suggested.

Indian Head Campground was located near Spinney Mountain Reservoir, which was a little smaller than Rampart Reservoir. It had trails for bike riding, hiking, and even horseback riding a few miles down the road. There was even an area to go white water rafting, which pleased Tyler. Having found the perfect campground with activities for everyone, the Thompson kids headed back to Manitou Springs to their aunt's gallery, where they found her waiting for them.

"Well, it's about time," she said. "We should have already left for the airport."

"Don't worry. The airlines are never on time," Tyler told his aunt.

After they got into their aunt's station wagon and merged onto the interstate, Aunt Marybeth asked how they had made out.

"We found the perfect campground," Stephanie answered. "There are bike paths, horseback riding trails, a volleyball court, and swimming."

"Don't forget fishing," Steve said.

"Yeah, and not too far from the campground, I can go white water rafting if I want to," Tyler said. "I just wish I could talk someone into going with me," he added, nudging his brother.

"Maybe Alex would like to go with you," Aunt Marybeth said.

Tyler beamed at the idea; he had forgotten about his cousin, who he had been rafting with a few years ago.

"I forgot that Alex likes to go rafting," he said.

Not much was said during the rest of the way to Denver except for Tyler occasionally asking for help on a crossword puzzle he was doing. Stephanie was reading one of the books that she had found in the attic, and Steve had a headset on and was listening to a new CD that he had bought.

At the airport, the family soon learned that Tyler was right about the plane not being on time. They browsed through a gift shop while they waited. Stephanie picked out a fashion magazine and bought it.

"How do you think I would look with this haircut?" Stephanie asked her Aunt.

"Why would you want to change your hair?" Aunt Marybeth asked.

"I don't know, just to be different," she said.

As Aunt Marybeth was telling Stephanie that she thought her hair was pretty just the way it was, Tyler was standing near the window, watching the planes come in.

"I think his plane just came in," he said as he looked out at a Delta 747.

Sure enough, he found out that he was right. The attendant announced the arrival of Flight 367 from Los Angeles. As Alex arrived from the long concourse, his aunt and niece greeted him with hugs.

"Where are Tyler and Steve?" Alex asked.

"Why, they were just here," Aunt Marybeth said, turning around.

But when they looked around, the boys were nowhere to be found.

"What if they got kidnapped?" Aunt Marybeth said frantically.

"Surely, someone would have seen them," Alex said, trying to calm his aunt down.

"Yeah, they probably just went to get a snack or something," Stephanie said.

The three of them had started a search for the two boys when they suddenly appeared.

"I just saw one of the men who had been chasing me!" Tyler said. "He was carrying a large flat suitcase and got on a plane to New York."

Chapter 3
Close Encounter

"You two had me worried sick," Aunt Marybeth said with a frown. "So he got on a plane to New York. There's no crime in that."

"Yeah, but don't you see, New York is known for its art, and he was carrying a suitcase that probably had stolen pictures in it to sell to some big art gallery," Tyler said.

"Who are you talking about?" Alex asked, confused.

"Oh, it's just a bunch of nonsense," Aunt Marybeth said. "Come on, let's get Alex's bags so we can go home."

On the way to the baggage claim, the teenagers took turns telling Alex about the robberies and about Tyler getting chased. Aunt Marybeth didn't say anything but had a disapproving look on her face. As they started home, the conversation changed to the big camping trip only a few days away.

"We found a great place to go camping," Steve told his cousin.

Alex had not been informed about the camping trip that his cousins had been planning for months. As they filled him in, he became more and more excited. He loved to go camping and seldom got the chance.

"Do you still like to go white water rafting?" Tyler asked him.

"Yeah, I sure do," Alex answered. "It's been a long time since I've had the opportunity to go rafting."

"Okay, we're here." Aunt Marybeth said as she pulled into a parking lot.

"We're where?" Stephanie asked her Aunt, puzzled.

"Casa Bonita," Aunt Marybeth said.

But the kids still didn't know where they were.

"Is this a Mexican restaurant?" Tyler asked.

"Yes, a unique Mexican restaurant," she answered.

They soon saw that their Aunt was right. After getting their food, they found seats in the middle of a jungle-type setting. Their table overlooked a pool with boulders on the backside and a high diver was doing a back flip from the boulders into the pool. Everyone cheered as the diver splashed into the water. After a few more dives, she took a break.

"This place is neat," Alex said. "How did you find out about it?"

"A friend of mine brought me here for lunch one day," Aunt Marybeth said as the next act started.

The next act was three singing and dancing bears. They sang and joked around, including the audience in their comedy routine.

"We need an assistant from the audience," one of the bears said. "Will anyone volunteer?"

"How about you, Miss?" the other bear said, talking to Aunt Marybeth. "Would you be so kind to join us?"

"Well, I don't know," Aunt Marybeth started to say, but with her nephews and niece cheering her on, she couldn't say no.

Aunt Marybeth assisted the bears in several magic tricks. For the first trick, she examined a top hat to prove that it was a normal hat. Then, the bears pulled two rabbits out of the hat. For the final act they made her disappear in a magic chamber, and then she reappeared. The bears gave her a scarf that they had used in one of their magic tricks.

"You looked great up there," Stephanie told her aunt when she joined them.

"I have to admit, the kid in me really had a lot of fun," Aunt Marybeth said.

After a short break the next act featuring two mimes started. It was difficult to understand what they were saying at first, but after a few minutes, all four teenagers were bursting with laughter.

"That was a fun place," Stephanie said as they were leaving the restaurant.

"Yeah, we should bring Mom and Dad next time," Tyler said.

During the drive home the kids talked about horseback riding, fishing and outdoor activities. It had been awhile since the Thompson kids had seen their cousin, so they talked about their last visit when they went camping near Rocky Mountain National Park.

"Remember when we scared you into thinking that we saw a bear," Steve said to Stephanie.

"I was just a kid then," she protested.

"You're still a kid," Tyler teased.

"Well, this time when we're camping, you're not going to scare me with any bear stories," she said.

Steve winked at Alex with a look that said, "We'll see."

The next day they went shopping for camping gear in Colorado Springs. Since Alex hadn't known about the planned outing, he had to buy a new sleeping bag.

"The sleeping bag that I have is old anyway, and before I leave I can just mail the new one home," he said, as he picked out the one that he wanted.

The teenagers also bought extra kerosene, fishing lures, and some snacks. When they were done shopping, they headed back to their aunt's house. After unloading the truck, they sat down in front of the television. They were changing channels when a special report came on. They learned that during the night there had been another robbery at one of the Galleries in Manitou Springs, the Rose Gallery.

"I think Aunt Marybeth knows the owners," Stephanie said as she picked up the phone to call her aunt, who was working in her gallery.

"Yes, I already heard about the robbery. The owners are good friends of mine," she said sadly.

"The robber couldn't have been the man that got on the plane," Steve said after Stephanie had hung up.

"It is possible that the man returned from New York the same day he left," Tyler said. "And besides, there were two other men who chased me and either of them could have robbed the gallery."

Everyone agreed with Tyler but still wondered if the men who had chased Tyler were really connected to the robberies or could they be innocent.

"Why don't we go to the Rose Gallery and look for clues?" Steve suggested.

"Yeah, they will probably let us since the owners know Aunt Marybeth," Stephanie said.

The teenagers climbed in their aunt's truck and headed to Manitou Springs. They arrived at their aunt's gallery a few minutes later.

"What are you kids up to?" she asked.

"We thought we would go by your friends' gallery and see if we can find any clues," Tyler told his aunt.

"I'm sure the police have done a thorough job," Aunt Marybeth said, "but I was thinking about visiting them. Perhaps I should go with you."

After Aunt Marybeth asked her associate, June, to watch over the store, they headed to the Rose Gallery. The gallery was only a few blocks away so they decided to walk.

As they entered the gallery, a short, gray-haired woman greeted them.

"Hi, Marybeth! It's so good to see you," she said.

"Rosalie, you remember my niece and nephews," she said as she introduced them. "And this is another nephew of mine from California, Alex."

"Rosalie, oh, the gallery must be named after you," Stephanie said.

"Why yes, my dear, sweet husband, John, named it," she answered as she put her arm around the man beside her.

The man smiled and gave Aunt Marybeth a hug.

"We heard about the theft," Aunt Marybeth said.

"I hope they nail those crooks!" John said, irritation in his voice.

"We hope so too. That's why we're here. We were hoping that you would let us look around for clues," Tyler said.

"You kids are welcome to, but I don't think you'll find anything. Even the police didn't find much," John said.

While the adults sat and drank some espresso that John had made, the teenagers looked around the antique shop. The gallery contained beautiful scenic pictures, which Stephanie took an immediate liking to.

"Look at this ocean picture. It's so beautiful," Stephanie said to her brothers.

"That looks like a place close to where I live," Alex told his cousins.

The Thompson kids had never been to the ocean and the brothers admired the picture as much as their sister did. As they daydreamed about seeing the ocean someday, they also scouted for clues. But after a couple of hours, they finally decided that there wasn't one clue to be found. After saying good-bye to John and Rosalie, they headed back to Aunt Marybeth's gallery.

During the drive back, Aunt Marybeth told them that the burglar alarm had gone off at the gallery but the thieves had gotten away before the cops arrived.

"Boy, the thieves must really know what they are doing to have avoided getting caught," Tyler commented.

The next morning over breakfast, the kids planned what they would do that day. The boys wanted to go fishing, but Stephanie wanted to visit Miramont Castle. Since they would get to do plenty of fishing on their camping trip, Stephanie persuaded Steve to visit the castle with her, but Tyler had other plans.

"I thought I would go by the library and read up on Bruce Duncan," he told them.

Alex decided to hang out with Tyler at the library. The castle didn't interest him much.

"It's not like a real castle or anything," he said. "Ireland has some real castles."

"You've been to Ireland?" Tyler asked.

As Alex told his cousin all about his trip to Ireland, Steve and Stephanie went into Miramont Castle.

Together they walked through the castle, trying to picture what it must have been like in the 1800's. Their favorite room was the Drawing Room with a gold ceiling and a large sandstone fireplace.

"I could sit in that room for hours," Stephanie told her brother.

After they had walked through the castle, they went to the miniature museum, which contained a large collection of antique toys and dolls. Stephanie always enjoyed this part of the castle, but to Steve it was very boring.

"Come on, Stephanie, let's go to the train museum," he said as they stepped outside the castle.

They were about to head toward the separate building that was used for the train display when Steve pulled his sister aside.

"Wait," he whispered.

"Don't you want to see the trains?" she said, annoyed.

"Look!" Steve pointed. "That man over there, he's the same man we saw at the airport!"

Stephanie looked in the direction that Steve was pointing to see a man walking toward the castle.

"Are you sure he's the same man you saw?" Stephanie asked.

"I am sure that he's the same guy. I want to find out what he is doing here," Steve said.

"He seems to be in a hurry," Stephanie said.

The kids ran to catch up with the man who was going into the castle. They watched him pay his admission to get in and then briskly walk through the foyer. The teens would have to pay admission again to get back into this part of the attraction. They looked through their pockets but didn't have enough! If only Tyler were there. He had the extra money.

"Maybe if we ask the attendant really nice, he'll let us back in," suggested Stephanie.

After asking the attendant, they found it was no use. They waited outside for the man to come out.

"That man doesn't appear to be someone who would enjoy visiting museums alone," Stephanie commented.

"He is definitely up to something," Steve agreed. "After all, he practically ran inside."

"Maybe he was running away from someone," Stephanie said.

"That's the only logical reason that I can think of," Steve agreed. "If someone had been chasing him they never would have guessed he went into a museum."

Just as the teen detectives were discussing the possibilities, they noticed a gray BMW driving very slowly nearby. The man behind the wheel had dark hair and seemed to be looking for someone.

"Look at the guy in the gray BMW," Steve whispered to Stephanie.

"He looks suspicious," his sister agreed.

"Darn, I didn't get the license plate number," Steve said right after the car drove out of sight. "What do we do now?" Stephanie asked.

"We just have to wait," Steve replied. "At least Tyler should be here soon."

They were still watching for the man to come back out of the museum when their brother and Alex pulled up. Steve and Stephanie got in the truck and filled them in on what had happened.

"We would have gone back inside," Stephanie said, "but we didn't have enough money to get back in."

"How long has he been in there?" Tyler asked.

"About thirty-five minutes," Stephanie replied.

"He should be coming out soon. Let's wait in the car," Tyler said.

As the teens waited in the truck, Tyler told them that he hadn't learned anything at the library.

"I found several articles about Bruce Duncan, but they all had the same information. He started painting when he was ten and grew up in Colorado Springs."

"Look! There he is!" Steve interrupted.

The man came out of the castle and was headed for the parking lot.

"That's not the man we saw at the airport," Tyler said. "For one thing, he's wearing glasses."

"Lots of people wear both glasses and contacts," Stephanie pointed out.

The man got into a blue pickup truck and pulled out of the parking lot. Even though Tyler didn't think he was the same man, he decided to follow him.

"Alex, write down his license plate number, just in case," he told his cousin, who was seated next to him.

The man headed off Ruxton Avenue to Main Street. After he passed the town clock, he slowed down.

"Do you think he saw us?" Stephanie asked.

"It's a good possibility," Tyler said. "He's been watching in his mirror the whole time."

"Look, he's stopping in front of Aunt Marybeth's gallery!" Tyler exclaimed.

The teens decided to park behind a row of cars and watch him. The man didn't get out of the car but sat there as if he were waiting for someone.

A few minutes later two men walked out of Aunt Marybeth's gallery. They got in the pickup truck and talked for a few minutes. As the truck pulled away from the curb, one of the men looked right at the teenagers. Tyler was certain they had seen them, but decided to continue following them. He was staying close behind when all of a sudden a large truck pulled out from nowhere.

"Look out!" Stephanie yelled.

Chapter 4
Robbed

Tyler jerked the steering wheel to the left to avoid hitting the truck, which he just missed by inches.

"Boy, it's a good thing that no one was on my left!" he said as he pulled over to the side of the road to catch his breath. "That car is gone now."

The teens headed back to their aunt's gallery. They were anxious to know what the men were doing there. At the shop, their aunt told them the men had been inquiring about Bruce Duncan paintings.

"What did you tell them?" Tyler asked.

"I told them that we didn't have any," she said.

"I thought that you had..." Stephanie started to say.

"I do," her aunt interrupted. "But I didn't want those guys to know. They were making me too nervous."

The teens were telling their aunt about seeing the guy at the castle, when Tyler suddenly remembered he was supposed to be somewhere.

"I just remembered something," he said. "Alex and I will be right back."

Tyler motioned to Alex and the two of them rushed out the door. He explained about the men whom he had overheard talking yesterday. They had said they would meet again at the fountain at exactly this time. But when they arrived at the fountain a few minutes later, no one was there. They were too late!

He drove back to the gallery and walked in with a long face. He explained why they had rushed out.

"At least we got their license plate number, if they are the same men that we just saw," Stephanie reminded him.

Tyler brightened. "I'll call Officer Johnston right now and have him follow up on it."

"While you're at it, why don't you let him solve the mystery," Aunt Marybeth said.

Aunt Marybeth didn't like the fact that they were following people and being chased. She knew they could get themselves in danger. She was glad that they would soon be going camping and suggested that they call their friends and find out when they could expect them.

First, Tyler called Officer Johnston, who promised to check on the license plate number and get back to them. Then, he called Dylan, who would be driving himself, his younger brother Andrew, and Stephanie's best friend, Kamryn, to Manitou Springs. When he got off the phone, he told them that they still planned to leave Friday morning.

Stephanie decided to call Kamryn also, even though she knew when she would be arriving.

"See you in a day and a half," she said after talking several minutes.

"Now that your plans are set, Friday morning before you leave, you can stop by The Bait Shop and pick up the boat you'll be taking," Aunt Marybeth told them after they hung up with their friends.

"You rented a boat for us?" Steve asked, surprised.

Aunt Marybeth just smiled, indicating that she had. All four teenagers were soon giving her hugs.

"We already have our fishing poles ready," Stephanie commented.

"What do you mean *our* fishing poles? Who said anything about you coming fishing?" Stephanie's twin brother teased.

"I can fish just as well as you can," Stephanie said, defending herself.

After dinner the family sat in the living room. Aunt Marybeth was doing crochet, Tyler and Alex were playing chess and both Steve and Stephanie were reading. The room was so quiet that Aunt Marybeth jumped when the phone rang. She answered it to find out that it was Officer Johnston for Tyler.

The whole room was quiet as the family listened closely to Tyler talking with the officer. They wanted to know what was going on, but it was hard to tell with Tyler not saying much. When he hung up the phone, they all immediately started asking him questions.

"Give me a second, and I'll tell you what he said," he told them.

Tyler explained that the car belonged to a Brian Miller, who had no criminal record. What he didn't tell them was that the officer, like his aunt, thought that these robberies were too dangerous for them. Maybe he was right, Tyler thought, as he headed for bed.

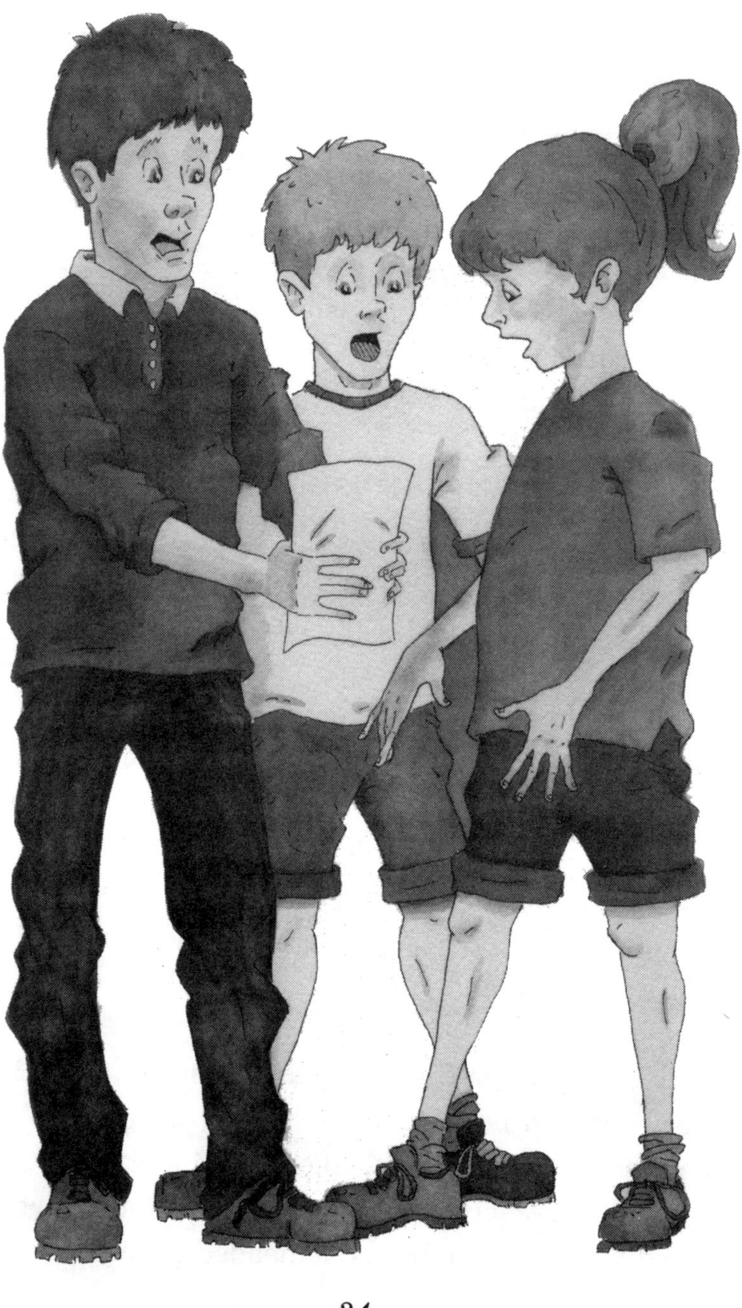

The next couple of days seemed to drag on forever as the teens anxiously waited for Friday to arrive. When it was finally Friday, they woke up to the smell of pancakes and sausage. After eating breakfast, Tyler and Steve went to pick up the boat that Aunt Marybeth had rented for them. When they returned they loaded the truck with their camping supplies.

"I wish they would get here," Tyler said when they were done packing.

Soon the doorbell rang, and all four teenagers rushed to the door in anticipation.

But when they opened the door they were surprised to find no one was there. Instead, there was a small unaddressed envelope on the doormat.

Tyler picked up the envelope and opened it. The inside note was very short and to the point.

"STay ouT of our way, or else!"

The teenagers stared at the note in silence. Who could it be from? And what did it mean; or else?

Aunt Marybeth had been downstairs doing laundry when the doorbell rang.

"Where are your friends?" she asked when she came up the stairs. "I thought I heard the doorbell ring."

"Uh, it was just a salesperson." Tyler said quickly before anyone could say anything. He didn't want to worry their aunt.

"Hey, they're here." Steve, who had been looking out the window, said.

In all of the excitement of leaving for Indian Head Campground, the kids seemed to have forgotten all about the note, all except Stephanie. The note made her nervous. While the others were setting up their tents, she was sitting by herself on a log.

"Stephanie, are you going to help?" Tyler asked. "After we get our tents up, we can go for a hike."

Kamryn joined Stephanie on the log and asked her what was wrong. That's when she told her about the note. Kamryn gasped when she told her what the note said.

"Do you think we are being watched right now?" Kamryn asked.

"I don't know what to think," Stephanie answered.

"I can't believe that you guys were threatened," Kamryn said aloud to Stephanie and her brothers.

"What is she talking about?" Dylan asked.

Tyler filled their friends in on the note that had been left on the doormat.

"It is probably just a prank," Steve said.

The other boys agreed with Steve.

"Don't worry about it, Steph, we're here to camp and have fun," Tyler said.

The teenagers decided to take a long hike through the woods, marking their trail as they went so they could find their way back. It was too early in the day to see very many animals except for the chipmunks. After walking a couple of hours, the kids stopped to rest on some boulders.

"When we are done with our hike, we can go back to camp for some hot dogs and baked beans, and then we can take the boat out on the lake," Tyler said.

"It will be fun to do some lake fishing for a change," Alex said. "All I do at home is salt-water fish."

"We can work on our tans, as long as the sun is still out," Kamryn said to Stephanie.

"Yeah," Stephanie answered, her thoughts still on the note. But as the day went on, she too was able to put the threatening note out of her mind.

After the teenagers had finished their lunch of hot dogs and beans, Stephanie suggested roasting marshmallows.

Then, the kids launched the boat into the reservoir. Stephanie caught the first fish, a small trout.

"Oh, that figures," Steve said with envy.

"Didn't think I could fish, huh?" she asked smiling back.

It had been awhile since Stephanie had been fishing with her brothers. Her father had given her some pointers since then at a church outing that they had gone to. He showed her how to cast her line out better and to bait her hook.

Tyler was the next one to catch a fish, a big bass.

"I know what we'll be eating tonight," he smiled.

They caught a few more fish and then headed back to their campsite where they cleaned and cooked the fish for dinner.

The next day the teens started their day riding horses. After they had been riding for a couple of hours, Tyler looked at his watch and said they better head back.

Suddenly, Stephanie stopped her horse and told the others to stop. In the nearby woods, she could see a small fawn watching them in the distance. But when all of the horses stopped, the fawn took off out of sight.

"What did you see, Stephanie?" Tyler asked.

"A cute deer," she answered.

"Oh, too bad we didn't bring our shot guns up here with us," Steve said, teasing his sister.

"You wouldn't dare! Shoot a cute, helpless fawn?" Stephanie said.

"Ok, I'll shoot it with my camera," Steve smiled.

"Oh, that would be so cute. I also brought my camera and my tripod," Kamryn, who also shared Steve's hobby of photography, said.

"I got a special lens for night photography for my birthday last year, maybe we can try it out later," Steve said.

At the time, Steve had no idea that he would have the perfect opportunity to try out his new lens that night. As all seven of them were sitting around the campfire talking, a deer passed right in front of them. Steve got his camera from his tent and began snapping away. He had only taken a couple of pictures when the deer ran off.

"Darn, the flash scared him away," Steve said.

"You should make sure your night lens is ready for next time," Tyler said.

Sure enough, Tyler had been right. The very next night; several deer walked by the campsite. The teenagers had almost missed seeing them in the dark, but the light from the campfire illuminated them. Steve grabbed his camera, which was close by, and began taking pictures. He had used up almost a whole roll of film before the deer dashed off.

Over the next few days, the teenagers spent their time fishing, swimming, riding rented bikes, and hiking through the woods. By the end of their camping trip, everyone was doing their own thing. Tyler went white water rafting with Alex while Steve, Dylan, and Andrew played basketball and catch. Stephanie and Kamryn mainly rode their bikes and played badminton. They were so busy having fun that they forgot all about the note and the robberies until they started packing up their camping gear.

"I wonder if there have been any more robberies," Stephanie said.

"Yeah, and if there have been any more mysterious notes delivered," Tyler said.

"If Aunt Marybeth got any notes, she'll be awfully worried," Steve said.

When they arrived back at Aunt Marybeth's house, they could tell right away that something was bothering her.

"What's wrong, Aunt Marybeth?" Stephanie asked.

"My gallery was robbed!" she told them.

Chapter 5
Vanished

The teenagers were in shock from the news. What could they possibly say to their aunt? Her gallery was her whole life.

There was silence for a few minutes before Tyler asked his aunt, "What happened to the night watchman?"

"Apparently, he got knocked out," she said. "When he came to, he didn't remember what had happened, as if he had been drugged."

"Do the police have any leads?" Steve asked.

"They said that they would run lab work on some fingerprints that were found around the cash register, which was broken into, but who knows if they will find anything?" their aunt replied.

"Why did it have to happen to you?" Stephanie asked her aunt as she gave her a big hug.

"I don't know, but I can't let it get me down," Aunt Marybeth replied.

Because of the circumstances, Dylan suggested that Andrew, Kamryn, and he leave early, even though they had permission to stay another week at Aunt Marybeth's house.

"No, I won't hear of it. If it wasn't for you kids here to

put some sunshine into my day, I would be lost," Aunt Marybeth said.

That night as the family had dinner together, there wasn't much said. After they had finished eating, Tyler pulled the others aside.

"We have to catch those robbers," he told them.

"Yeah," Steve agreed. "We may already know what the robbers look like."

"I still don't understand what makes you so sure that the men you saw were the thieves," Dylan said.

"It's just that they acted so suspicious. They must be up to something. If only we had more to go on," Tyler said.

"Maybe they left a clue behind at Aunt Marybeth's Gallery," Steve suggested.

"If they left any clues behind, surely the police would have found them," Stephanie reasoned.

The rest knew that Stephanie was right, but they still had to try. They made plans to search Aunt Marybeth's gallery the next day. They would divide the store up into areas for each one to search.

The next morning, all seven teenagers were up by the time Aunt Marybeth came down to the kitchen.

"Can I get you some coffee?" Tyler asked his weary-eyed aunt.

"That would be great, I didn't sleep too well last night," she said, yawning.

"Perhaps we should wait to clean up your store," Tyler said as he handed her the coffee. "It won't hurt if we wait another day."

Aunt Marybeth didn't put up any argument. She did-n't know if she could face her gallery just yet, anyway.

"We haven't taken a day just for fun since you kids got here," she said. "Why don't we spend the whole day together? Do you kids have any ideas about what you would like to do?"

"How about horseback riding in the Garden of the Gods?" Stephanie suggested.

Garden of the Gods was a beautiful park at the base of Pike's Peak. It had some spectacular views of the mountains along with magnificent red sandstone forma-tions. Even though the Thompson kids and their friends had all been to the park many times, they thought Stephanie's idea was a great one.

"We can take along a picnic lunch," Aunt Marybeth said, smiling.

When they reached the park, they stopped to take some group pictures standing in front of Balanced Rock, famous for its "balancing act" on top of a smaller rock. Balanced Rock has often been called the Eighth Wonder of the World.

"Look at those people climbing up that cliff," Steve said, pointing.

"That's scary, just watching," Andrew said.

They all headed for the stables where they were assigned horses. Tyler's horse was named Buttercup and was at the head of the line, Steve was in the middle riding Coca, Stephanie rode close behind on Twilight, and Aunt Marybeth was behind the three of them on Blazer.

Dylan, Andrew, Kamryn, and Alex rode their horses behind Aunt Marybeth. They waved to each other as they rode along the trail following the lead horse just in front of Tyler. The trail was a little rocky and Tyler wondered if it would be too much for his aunt, but as they turned the corner, he looked back to see her smiling and patting her horse. He and the others were all glad that she was able to put concerns about the gallery aside and have a good time. After they said good-bye to their horses and to the stable keepers, Aunt Marybeth suggested that they visit the zoo.

"Are you sure you are up to it?" Tyler asked.

"This is just what I needed," she said. "I don't even want to think about my gallery until tomorrow."

With that said, the Thompson kids and their friends headed to the Cheyenne Mountain Zoo where they had a lot of fun watching the animals. After the zoo they went out to dinner before heading home. It wasn't until much later that evening that Aunt Marybeth mentioned the gallery again.

"I think I better get some shut-eye," she said. "Tomorrow will be a long day cleaning up the gallery."

The next day the Thompson kids went to the gallery with their aunt. The thieves had taken the few Duncan paintings that were in the back room and a few different pieces in the front. It didn't make any sense to any of them why the thieves took different pieces of art and left others behind. The only logical reason that they could think of was that the robbers had run out of time.

The teenagers spent the morning helping their aunt clean up. There was glass all over the floor from the window that the thieves had broken to get in. As Aunt Marybeth swept up the glass, the teen detectives looked for clues. After a few minutes their aunt asked them what they were doing.

Tyler didn't say anything as he picked up a matchbook he had spotted on the floor. It was from a place called the Bear Creek Bottling Company. Quickly, he put it in his pocket before his aunt saw it.

"You kids don't need to be snooping around here all day," their aunt said. "Why don't you go swimming or go see a movie?"

The teenagers knew that their aunt was getting aggravated, so they decided to look for clues later. Tyler gave a wink to the others to indicate that they had better leave. They had just stepped outside the door when they saw the man who had come by the store a couple weeks before asking about Duncan paintings. He was walking straight toward the gallery.

The teens stepped back into the shop and told their aunt about the man coming down the street. Their aunt didn't say anything but, sure enough, the man came in the store.

"Why would he come back here?" Stephanie wondered.

"Pardon me," he said to Aunt Marybeth. "I seem to remember a painting you had the last time I was in here. It was of an old covered wagon out in the middle of a desert."

"Oh, I am sorry but that painting was stolen just last night," Aunt Marybeth replied.

"Stolen! How dreadful, I am so sorry." He started to leave but stopped for a second. "Wasn't the painting sitting over here next to this one?"

Aunt Marybeth nodded that he was right.

"Why would thieves steal that painting and leave this one behind? It is well known to be worth twice as much. The thieves obviously don't know much about art," the man said.

"How do you come to know so much about art?" Aunt Marybeth asked.

"Oh, I'm a collector," he said. "I am planning on starting a shop myself."

The man apologized for Aunt Marybeth's misfortune and left.

"And you guys thought he was a thief!" Aunt Marybeth remarked.

All of them had to admit that the man was very nice, but they were still suspicious of him, especially Tyler, who thought he was trying to cover up something. However, the man was right about the fact that the thieves did not know very much about art - or maybe they wanted it to appear that way.

Outside the gallery, the teenagers talked about what they would do for the rest of the afternoon.

"We could hang out at the arcade," Steve suggested.

"Or the mall," Stephanie added.

"I just want to find the thieves," Tyler said.

"But, what can we do?" Stephanie asked.

"For one thing, we can check out all of the galleries that got robbed," Tyler said. "I made a list from the articles in the paper, and I thought we could go to each one."

Everyone quickly agreed and it was decided that they would start with the shops in Colorado Springs that were robbed.

The first one was all boarded up so they looked around the outside but came up with nothing. Although the second shop was open, they didn't find any clues.

The teenagers told the owner that they were looking for clues leading them to the thieves.

"Well, if they left anything behind, I'm sure it's gone now," he said. "I had the whole place remodeled right after the robbery."

The group headed back to Manitou Springs, where they hoped their luck would be better.

The first gallery that they went into, the clerk wasn't too happy about them being there.

"I guess I can let you look around for a short while, but don't touch anything," he said.

The gallery had a lot of abstract art and valuable paintings locked in glass cases.

"I wonder what the artist was thinking when he painted this one," Stephanie said.

"He probably wasn't thinking about anything. It looks like he just threw some paint on the canvas," Steve commented.

Tyler was looking at another painting that was in a glass case.

"So that's what he looked like," Stephanie said as she read the inscription at the bottom: Bruce Duncan. The man looked to be very sturdy and had dark features. The look in his eyes seemed to ask, "What are you looking at?"

"His face looks very familiar but I don't know why," Stephanie said.

"He makes me nervous," Steve said, and then added, "so does that clerk watching us, let's look around and get out of here."

The teens gave up trying to find anything so they left the store. They were outside when Tyler said he wanted to get a business card and went back into the store.

"Can I get one of your business cards?" he asked the owner.

"Sure, help yourself," the man said, pointing to where they were.

As Tyler reached for a business card, a pen fell off the counter. He reached down to pick it up. As he looked at the pen, his eyes got bigger.

"Hey, mister. Can I keep this pen?" he asked.

"Sure, I guess so," he answered and went back to what he was doing.

Outside, Tyler showed his brother and sister what he had found.

"Arthur Duncan, Public Accountant," Tyler read aloud the writing on the pen. "I think that I remember reading that he was Bruce's brother."

"That's right, his twin brother!" Stephanie exclaimed.

"You don't have to get that excited," Steve teased.

"I just realized something," Stephanie explained. "Remember the drawing of Bruce Duncan that I showed you inside?"

"Yeah," Steve said.

"Well, I knew that the face looked familiar," Stephanie continued. "It looked just like the man in the gray BMW that drove by Miramont Castle."

"It could have been Arthur Duncan following the man who ran inside the castle," Steve said.

"This is getting interesting but, unfortunately, that was the last gallery on my list," Tyler said. "If only we had found more clues."

"Wait a minute," he thought. "What about the book of matches?" He pulled it out of his pocket.

"Hey, guys, look at this. I found it at Aunt Marybeth's. I had forgotten all about it until now," he exclaimed.

"The Bear Creek Bottling Company, 662 N. Mountainside Drive, Manitou Springs," Stephanie read.

"Maybe one of the robbers dropped it," Steve said.

"I know our chances are not good but what do we have to lose?" Tyler asked.

After having lunch, Tyler looked at the map for Mountainside Drive, and after locating it, they headed for the Bear Creek Bottling Company.

The company wasn't an easy place to find. Mountainside Drive was a long and winding road with buildings few and far between. After driving up and down the road for several minutes, they decided that there was no such number as 662. The closest house number they could find was number 664.

"It has to be before this house," Tyler reasoned. "I think I remember passing some old building a short ways back."

Tyler drove back to a spot where he saw an old building that was partially hidden by some trees.

"It looks like an old abandoned warehouse," Stephanie commented.

"This doesn't seem like much of a clue," Steve added. "That matchbook we found must have been old."

Tyler parked the truck and the teenagers got out and searched the area. In only a few minutes, Tyler found a sign hidden by a large bush. The letters were faded and they could barely make out the name, Bear Creek Bottling Company.

"This is the right place," Tyler called to the others. "Look at this sign I found."

"I don't think this is much of a clue after all. The place is abandoned," Steve said.

They were getting ready to leave when Tyler decided to drive around to the back of the building. Behind the building there was a blue Toyota pickup and a red Mercedes.

"Maybe there are people inside," Tyler said.

"Yeah, look, that door over there isn't boarded up," Steve said pointing.

Tyler parked the truck along the side of the building out of sight and turned off the engine. Quietly they crept out of the truck and walked toward the building. As they got closer, they could hear voices but they could not make out what was being said.

"It sounds like they are arguing," Steve whispered.

Tyler tried to peek through a knothole in one of the pieces of wood, but he could not see the men. This was discouraging at first, but as he looked closer, he thought he saw something even more incriminating.

"We have to call Officer Johnston, now!" he whispered to the others.

The teenagers tiptoed back to the truck where they pushed it out of earshot before starting it. As they drove off, Tyler explained that he had seen a row of paintings leaning against a back wall. Down the road a short ways, they found a pay phone to call the Manitou Springs Police Department.

"I was lucky to get a hold of Officer Johnston," Tyler commented as he drove back to the warehouse.

But when Tyler drove up to the warehouse, the teenagers soon found out that the phone call was too late. The cars that were parked in back were gone, and the door that the men had used to get into the building had been boarded up again. The men were nowhere to be found!

Chapter 6
Missing Suspects

"Where did they go?" Tyler asked aloud. Unfortunately, no one knew why the men left or where they went. Maybe they had heard the kids earlier and decided that they better leave. Whatever reason they had for leaving, it was too late to find out what they had been up to.

"One of us should have stayed behind to keep an eye on them," Steve said, frowning.

"Even if one of us had stayed behind, there wouldn't have been anything we could have done when they left," Tyler said. "We'll just have to keep an eye on this place."

"What will we tell Officer Johnston?" Stephanie asked quickly when she saw a police car driving up the road.

"We can tell them our suspicions and about the paintings that Tyler saw leaning against the wall," Dylan pointed out.

After Tyler had related the story to the police officer, they walked around to the back of the building. There, they pointed out the door that the men had apparently used to get into the building. Tyler also showed the officer the knot in the wood where he was able to peek through to get a view of the paintings. Now, because it was dark inside the building, they couldn't see through the hole.

"Can you get a search warrant?" Tyler asked the officer.

"Possibly, but it'll take awhile to put through the paperwork," the officer replied.

On the drive back to Aunt Marybeth's house, the teenagers discussed what had happened.

"I can't believe we were so close to the men who could have been the thieves!" Andrew said.

"Yeah, if only we had heard what they were saying, maybe we would know where they went," Dylan added.

"Hey, that's it!" Tyler said, suddenly slamming on the brakes and turning the car around. "We might not be able to watch this place 24 hours, but I think I know how we can listen for at least a few hours."

Everyone in the car wanted to know what Tyler was talking about, but he wouldn't tell.

"You'll see," he said.

Tyler parked the car in the same spot as before and cautiously stepped around the back of the building to make sure that no one had returned. Then, he peeked into a window near the door and was able to open it a little.

All of the teenagers got out of the car and walked over to where Tyler was standing near the window. Tyler had managed to open the window wide enough to get his hand inside.

"Do you think you can open it all the way?" Steve asked his brother.

"It's probably Tina," Stephanie said as she went to answer it.

"Oh, hi, Dad," Stephanie said.

"Well, don't try to sound too happy to hear from me," Jack Thompson said.

"Of course, I am glad to hear from you, Dad," she said. "I was just expecting to hear from someone else."

After they each had a chance to tell their parents about their detective work, they handed the phone to Aunt Marybeth.

"No, Jack. I don't think the kids are in any danger," she told him. "I think the police have this mystery about cleared up."

As Aunt Marybeth hung up the phone, it rang again and this time it was Tina.

"Just a minute," Aunt Marybeth said, handing the phone to Stephanie.

"Hi, Tina. What time can we..." Stephanie started to ask Tina. "Tina, calm down, what's wrong?"

Stephanie talked to her friend for several minutes before hanging up the phone.

"Well, what's up?" Tyler asked impatiently.

"It seems that Arthur Duncan has disappeared," Stephanie said. "He hasn't shown up for work and no one has heard from him in the last three days."

∾

Chapter 7
A Possible Clue

As the teenagers finished their game of Trivial Pursuit, they all wondered what had happened to Arthur Duncan. They hoped that their new friend's uncle was alright.

"Maybe if we went to his house, we could get a clue of his whereabouts," Tyler said. "Do you think Tina would have a key to get in?"

"Maybe, I'll call her back right now and find out," Stephanie said, picking up the phone.

"I don't have a key, but I know where one is hidden," Tina said. "I am just not sure that we should be doing this."

"Look at it this way: maybe we can find a clue to tell us where your uncle is," Stephanie said.

Tina agreed, and it was decided that the teens would meet the next morning and head over to her uncle's house. When they arrived at Arthur Duncan's house, Tina found the key hidden underneath a rock near the back door. Once inside the teenagers split up in different directions and began their search for clues.

"What are we looking for?" Tina asked.

"Anything that might tell us where your uncle went in a hurry, or maybe an old phone bill that will show who your uncle has been in contact with," Tyler said.

Steve looked at the pictures on the walls. There were several that were painted by Bruce Duncan. He wondered why he would steal more when he already had his personal collection. The teen sleuths searched each room one at a time, but they didn't find anything out of the ordinary. Stephanie even looked in the refrigerator, which had hardly any food.

"If we go by the food supply, it looks like he wasn't planning on being home for some time," she commented.

"Maybe he didn't have a chance to get to the store," Kamryn said.

"Or maybe Stephanie is right that he knew that he was going to be gone for a long time," Tyler said as he picked up a piece of paper.

"There's a phone number written down for Mountainside Lodge in Leadville. I think I'll call the phone number and see if he is registered as a guest."

Tyler dialed the number and waited for the clerk to look up Arthur Duncan.

"Is he all right?" Tyler asked the woman after listening to her reply for a few minutes.

"What's the matter?" Tina asked immediately after Tyler had hung up.

"He was a guest but was rushed to the hospital about three days ago," Tyler said. "They think he may have had a heart attack."

"Oh, no," Tina said. "I hope he is okay."

"They said he was admitted to St. John's," Tyler said. "We'll call there and find out his condition."

"I'll call since he is my uncle," Tina said.

While Tina talked to the nurse, the Thompson kids were left in suspense. They knew how serious a heart attack could be since a friend from their church passed away after having one.

Tina hung up the phone and let out a long sigh. "It turns out that he didn't have a heart attack after all," she said.

"What happened?" Steve asked.

"The doctors found a substance in his system that made it appear that he had a heart attack," Tina said.

"Do you mean he was poisoned?" Stephanie gasped.

"It appears so," Tina said. "Unfortunately, he is in a coma now so they can't ask him any questions."

"That's awful!" Tyler said. "I hope he will recover."

"I think I better go home and tell my parents the news," Tina said. "I am sure they will want to go visit him."

After dropping Tina off at her home, the teenagers headed to their aunt's art gallery where they filled their aunt in on Arthur Duncan.

"That's terrible! First, it looks like Arthur Duncan is the thief, and now he is poisoned," she said.

"Whoever tried to poison him must have had a good reason," Tyler said, "like they wanted to stop him from witnessing."

"Unfortunately, he's in a coma so we can't ask him any questions," Steve said.

The next morning Tyler was up again before everyone else. He was drinking orange juice and sitting by the
phone when his aunt entered the kitchen.

"Is something wrong?" she asked him. "You look like
you have something on your mind."

"I just tried calling Officer Johnston but he wasn't
in," he said. "I wanted to find out if they had learned
anything new on the case."

The teens hung out all morning waiting for the police
officer to call them back. Finally, the phone rang right
before noon.

"Hi, Tyler, I'm glad you called," the officer said. "You
gave us a great lead. We went into the building early
this morning, and as we suspected, all of the stolen art
was inside."

"Were you able to get fingerprints?" Tyler asked.

"Yes, and we have already analyzed them to learn
that none of them match our criminal files, so that means
we need more help from you," the officer explained.

"Since you're the only ones who saw the possible
suspects, we need detailed descriptions for some police
sketches," Officer Johnston told Tyler.

"We'll come right down to the police station," Tyler
said to him.

"I'm coming with you kids," Aunt Marybeth said after
Tyler filled her and the others in on their conversation.

At the station the teenagers described the men as best
they could. They also promised to keep an eye out for the
men and Officer Johnston gave Tyler his pager number.

"If you see anything suspicious or if you think you see any of the men, beep me immediately," the officer said.

The teen detectives were excited about their part in the case. That afternoon, they decided that they would go down by the fountain in case the men were meeting there.

The outdoor arcade area was close to the fountain so the teens took turns playing video games and watching for the thieves. It was starting to get dark when they gave up for the day. After grabbing a bite to eat at one of their favorite diners, they decided to go to the movies and then to the mall.

"Let's try to enjoy our day and do something fun," Tyler said after several hours of watching for the thieves.

"We can still keep an eye out for the men wherever we go," Stephanie added. "You never know, the thieves might be here right now."

"At the mall?" Tyler laughed.

"Sure, they go shopping just like us," Kamryn stood up for her friend. Secretly, she doubted that they would see any thieves at the mall or at any of their hangouts.

Kamryn's intuition was right. The teenagers didn't spot any of the men during the next few days. Before long it was time for Kamryn, Andrew, and Dylan to head home to Buena Vista.

"Well, we didn't catch any thieves, but we had a lot of fun," Andrew said.

"We'll let you know what happens," Tyler said as they waved good-bye.

The next day, Alex and Tyler decided to go rafting down the Colorado River. Since Alex would be leaving in a few short days also, they decided to make a day of it. They were both up at the crack of dawn and gone before anyone woke up. They left a note that said they wanted to get an early start.

Stephanie tried calling Tina to find out if there was any news on her uncle but there was no answer.

"They are probably still in Leadville," Stephanie said. "I left a message. Maybe she'll call me later."

"So what are we going to do all day?" Steve asked his sister.

"Beats me, I don't know what's left. We've been to the arcade, the mall, the movies, and roller skating," she answered.

The twins decided to spend most of their day outside playing catch and reading. Stephanie sat outside on the deck in her bathing suit, trying to get some sun. She was reading one of her new books that Aunt Marybeth had given her when Steve came up behind her and sprayed her with the hose. She wrestled to get the hose out of his hand and twisted it toward her brother. Now they were both soaking wet.

"You want to go swimming?" Steve asked his sister, laughing.

"Sure, but it's a long walk to the pool," Stephanie reminded him.

But neither of them minded the walk as they always walked a lot where they lived. Buena Vista was a small town so they often walked from their school to their friends' houses. On the walk back to Aunt Marybeth's house, they stopped for ice cream.

"You know we are going to spoil our dinner," Stephanie said.

"Nah, this is just a small snack," Steve answered.

But that night at dinner neither of them had second helpings of spaghetti and meatballs.

"Are you kids feeling okay?" Aunt Marybeth asked, a little worried.

"We're just not hungry," Steve said.

"It's probably because you ate too much ice cream," Tyler said.

"How did you know we had ice cream?" Stephanie asked her brother.

Tyler shrugged his shoulders. "The stain on Steve's shirt was my first clue. It looks like chocolate but that's just a guess."

"You're getting to be a really good detective," Stephanie said, smiling.

"Well, no ice cream for you two after we play miniature golf," Aunt Marybeth said.

"Miniature golf, that sounds like fun," Steve said, dismissing the ice cream.

But later that night after playing miniature golf, it didn't take much convincing for Stephanie and Steve to have ice cream with the others.

Soon it was time for Alex to fly back home. After the family said good-bye to him at the airport the next day; they headed to Aunt Marybeth's gallery.

"You can just drop me off at the gallery and then do whatever you kids want to do," Aunt Marybeth said.

"We thought we would just hangout with you for the day," Tyler said.

They were actually hoping that they could find a clue that they had missed at the gallery. They were snooping around there when Aunt Marybeth suggested that they go visit a friend of hers.

"Since the police are holding my stolen paintings for evidence, I feel better," she said. "Let's get out of here for the afternoon. June can handle the gallery."

The teens were reluctant to visit Aunt Marybeth's friend because it sounded boring. Lucky for them they didn't have to say anything; their aunt could tell their hesitation.

"What if I told you that her shop had been broken into also?" their aunt asked.

"Really, I mean - that's awful," Steve said. "We would love to come with you."

"That's good because I thought we could have lunch at that new pizza place in town that you kids have wanted to go to," Aunt Marybeth said smiling.

Steve and Stephanie had heard about the pizza place just the day before and had wished they had tried it while their friends were still in town. Still, they were excited over the news. At the restaurant, diners could watch the chef make the pizza crust by throwing it up in the air. Then, they got to build their own pizza by choosing the toppings and placing them on the pizza. The pizza was then placed in the oven.

The kids put together three large pizzas. One was a meat lover's pizza, the second had their favorite toppings of ham and pineapple, and the third pizza was a vegetable combo. After eating all the pizza they could, the four went to see Aunt Marybeth's friend, Jacqueline, who was surprised to see them.

"Why it's Marybeth Thompson, and you brought your nephews and niece!"

During the drive to see her friend, Aunt Marybeth had told them all about Jacqueline. She had been born and raised in France. She married an American and moved to Colorado with him. When her husband died, a few years ago, Jacqueline was left alone with no family. She loved Colorado so she stayed, but it was a treat when someone came to visit.

"Sorry that I haven't gotten over here before now," Aunt Marybeth said, "with the robbery and everything."

"Your shop got broke into also?" Jacqueline asked.

"Yes, it was robbed just this past week," Aunt Marybeth replied.

"Hopefully, the police will catch those thieves soon," Jacqueline commented.

"The police are on the case," Marybeth said. "My niece and nephews here actually helped them find all of the stolen merchandise that the police are holding for evidence."

"Wow, I'd love to hear how you were able to do that," Jacqueline said.

The teen detectives took turns explaining the events leading up to finding the hidden warehouse.

"That is great news!" Jacqueline said when they had finished. "I'm so glad that you came to visit, you really made my day."

After being polite and having tea with Aunt Marybeth and Jacqueline, the teens asked if they could look around.

"Of course you may," Jacqueline said. "You are such well-mannered kids."

Jacqueline's store, called the European Emporium, contained art and antiques from all over Europe. The teens enjoyed looking at the unique items.

"Look at this antique vase," Tyler said to his brother. "It looks like it should be in a museum. It must be over a hundred years old."

"That's nothing, look at this," Steve said, pointing to some kind of statue. "I don't even know what this is."

As the teenagers looked over the various paintings and antiques, Aunt Marybeth and Jacqueline caught up on old times. Before long, several hours had gone by.

"Wow, look at the time," Aunt Marybeth said. "We should be going soon."

But as Aunt Marybeth said this, Stephanie came across a clue.

"Look at this," she exclaimed. "It's Arthur Duncan's business card!"

Chapter 7
A Possible Clue

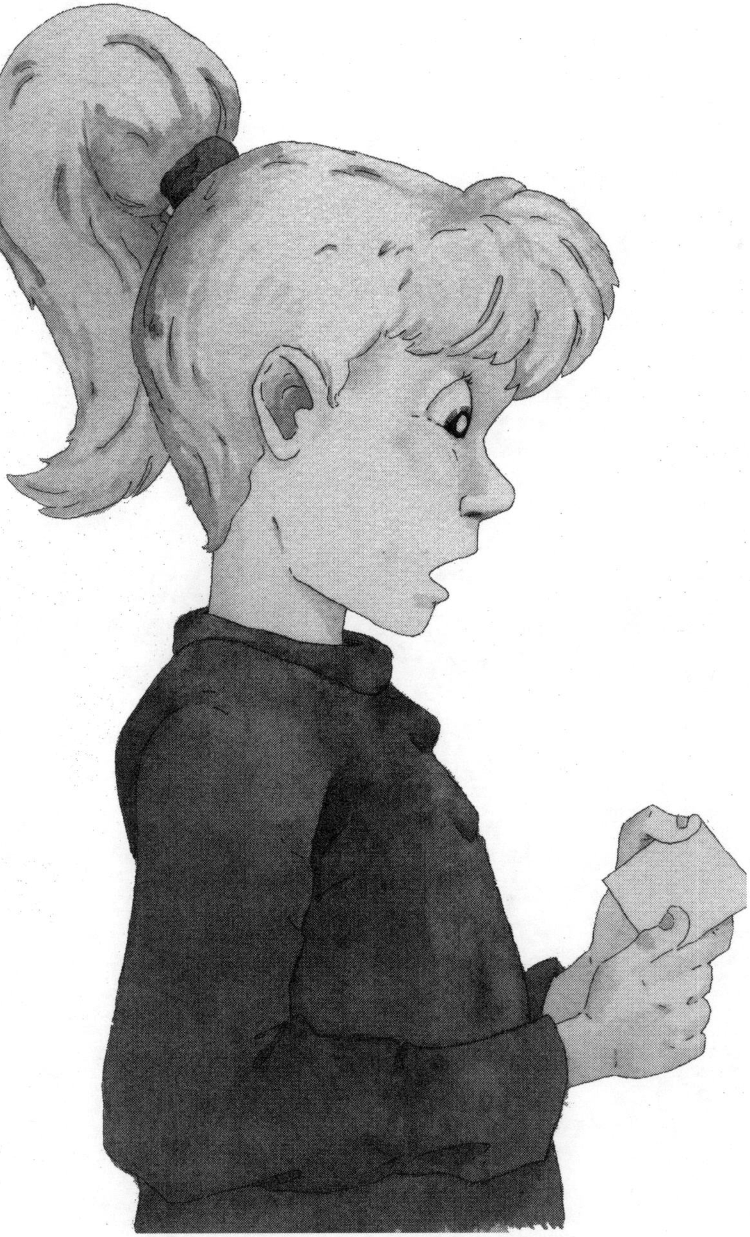

Chapter 8
Arrested

Stephanie picked up the business card lying on the floor and read aloud its contents.

"*Arthur Duncan, Public Accountant, 335 North Academy Boulevard, Colorado Springs, Colorado.*"

The teens described Arthur Duncan to Jacqueline, but she didn't remember anyone matching his description visiting her store.

"I don't pay much attention to most of the people who come by here," she said. "Why do you want to know?"

"We found his business card on the floor," Tyler said.

"And we have found other items with his name on them in a few other galleries that we visited," Stephanie said. "His innocence is sure looking slim."

"Remember that a man is innocent until proven guilty," Aunt Marybeth pointed out.

"Oh, we know," Steve said.

"Yeah, we are really hoping that he's not guilty," Stephanie said.

That night Aunt Marybeth took the kids out to a Melodrama Dinner Theater.

"I thought I would take you kids some place new," she said. "This place is always a lot of fun."

They sat at a long table with some other people and were served a family-style dinner. They ate barbecue ribs, fried chicken, corn on the cob, baked potatoes, and rolls for the main meal. Then, they had apple pie and pecan pie for dessert. At 8:30, the melodrama started. It was a lot of fun because audience participation was encouraged and following the melodrama was an old-fashioned sing-a-long.

The teens were laughing as they sang the old-fashioned tune, "My Bonnie Lies over the Ocean".

"My friends would laugh at me if they saw me now," Steve whispered to his twin sister.

"So would my friends," she added. "But I don't care. This is a lot of fun."

They were still laughing as they left the dinner theater.

Tyler stopped in the middle of the joke he was telling, "Hey, see that guy over there, it's one of the men that I overheard talking at the fountain."

"It looks like he is spying on us!" Steve said.

"And he must have good ears too because he just turned and ran away," Tyler exclaimed. "Come on, let's try to catch up with him."

The teens dashed through the crowd of people, but the man had disappeared. They didn't see him anywhere.

"Darn, we lost him," Tyler said.

Aunt Marybeth finally caught up with them, "What's the big idea, dashing off like that?"

Tyler explained about the man who they thought had been eavesdropping in on their conversation.

"He was probably just being nosey," Aunt Marybeth said.

"You're right," Tyler said quickly dismissing the subject. He had an uneasy feeling that the guy had actually been spying on them but he didn't want to worry his aunt.

The next morning after breakfast the teens headed back downtown. They were getting bored hanging out at the arcade and the fountain.

"Let's try to find some new places to go today," Stephanie suggested.

"Yeah, how about Michael Garman's Magic Town," her twin brother said. "We haven't been there on this visit yet."

Michael Garman's studio was another favorite place to visit for the Thompson kids. The gallery was full of bronze and hand-painted sculptures done by a local artist, Michael Garman. His work was very well known with some of his more popular sculptures being the aviator, soldier, and a fireman holding a little girl. The studio was in Old Colorado City, a town that bordered Manitou Springs.

The favorite part of the gallery for the Thompson kids was a section called Magic Town. It contained a whole block of three-dimensional characters and buildings complete with holograms that made some sculptures appear to be moving.

"This is so cool," Stephanie said.

"Look at the old-time diner scene, it looks so real," Tyler said.

"This block could be anywhere in the United States," Steve said.

"That's why they have named it, Anywhere, U.S.A." Stephanie said.

As the teens left the gallery and stepped outside, they realized that they had forgotten all about their investigation because they had been admiring the studio so much.

"We better get back to Manitou Springs, or we might miss seeing any of the men today," Tyler said.

On the way back, Tyler suddenly remembered the one place that they had forgotten to check for clues.

"We haven't been able to go into The Mystic Gallery because they have had it all boarded up," he said.

"That's right! It was one of the first places robbed," Stephanie said.

"And I just heard that they have recently reopened it," Steve continued.

Reaching town, the gallery was only a few blocks away. An older woman named Edith greeted them. She welcomed them to her gallery and was very cheerful until they mentioned the robbery, then her mood changed immediately.

"Simply dreadful! How could they do something like this to me? I have worked so hard and was getting ready to go on vacation, but now I can't afford the extra help so

I have to watch the store myself. I will also have to stay open late in hopes of making those extra sales," she said.

When the teens told her about the leads that the police had, and why they were there, her mood changed. She told them to search as long as they wanted and to let her know if there was anything she could do.

After searching only a few minutes, Steve called to the others.

"Hey, you guys, come over here, I found something," he said.

Tyler, Stephanie, and even Edith came over to see what he had found. It was an electric bill with Arthur Duncan's name and address on it!

"Maybe he dropped it while he was robbing the gallery," Stephanie commented.

"I doubt it, Sis," Tyler said. "If Arthur Duncan was guilty, he might accidentally drop something with his name on it in one of the shops, but in several galleries that were robbed. Why didn't the cops find this stuff?"

"It does seem more likely that he has been setup," Steve said.

"If this electric bill was here after the robbery, the police would have found it. I bet the real robbers decided that they need more evidence against him so they planted it here, later." Tyler said.

The three teenagers thanked Edith and left the gallery.

"What should we do now?" Stephanie asked Tyler.

"Let's go back to the Bear Creek Bottling Company and see if those men have returned," Steve suggested.

They headed over to the old warehouse where they found Officer Johnston in a stakeout nearby.

"Have you kids found anything yet?" the officer asked them.

Tyler showed him Arthur's business cards and the bill with his name on it.

He was about to tell the officer their theory about Arthur Duncan being set up when a special report came on the radio. It was an announcement that the Leadville Police had arrested Arthur Duncan!

Chapter 9
Spotted Again

"Wow, they must have nailed him right after he recovered in the hospital," Stephanie said. "I just talked to his niece, Tina, and there was still no change in his condition."

"We only heard the last part of the report. I'll call the station and find out the story," Officer Johnston said.

After talking for a few minutes with the dispatcher, the officer told the Thompson kids what he had learned.

"An old art gallery in Leadville was robbed and again only Bruce Duncan pieces were stolen," he said. "Not only that, but the witness gave the police an exact description of Arthur Duncan!"

"Wow! We were so sure that he was innocent," Tyler said.

"Even after all of the clues you found?" Officer Johnston asked, puzzled.

"That's what I was getting ready to talk to you about," Tyler said. "It just doesn't make any sense that he would accidentally drop a business card in every gallery, never mind an electric bill. Who carries around their electric bills? We think all of those clues were planted."

"Even on the cassette tape that we got, it sounded like he was being framed," Stephanie said.

"You kids would make good detectives," Officer Johnston said. "Unfortunately, it sounds like they have a cut-and-dry case against Arthur Duncan."

The teenagers headed back to their aunt's house where Stephanie phoned Tina, who answered on the first ring.

"Oh, hi," she said.

"Hi, we just heard the news..." Stephanie started to say.

"It's all a big mistake," Tina said. "When Uncle Arthur first came out of his coma he didn't remember anything. Now he remembers the real thieves poisoning him so that he wouldn't squeal on them."

"Does he remember anything else?" Stephanie asked.

"It turns out that he has been on the thieves' trail ever since the robberies started," Tina said. "He was spying on them right before they robbed the art gallery in Leadville."

"After all he has been through, he is the one to be arrested," Stephanie said.

"Yeah, but I am not too worried because my parents were with my uncle when he supposedly robbed the gallery," Tina said.

"We knew he wasn't guilty." Stephanie said. "We found some clues pointing to his innocence."

"Great!" Tina exclaimed. "My parents are trying to get him out of jail as we speak. I'm waiting to hear from them."

"Oh, we better not tie up the phone lines then," Stephanie said. "Will you call us if anything new develops?"

"Sure," Tina agreed.

Stephanie told Tina that they would continue looking for the real thieves.

"Boy, you kids are determined to solve this mystery," Aunt Marybeth said, as she had overheard the whole conversation. "What clues do you have?"

The teenagers each took turns explaining to their aunt why they thought Arthur Duncan was innocent. When they were done, she too thought he wasn't guilty.

"When he goes to trial, it has to be proven beyond a reasonable doubt that he is guilty," she said.

"We can help him there," Steve said.

After dinner the teenagers watched television waiting for Tina or Officer Johnston to call. It wasn't until about 8:00 when Tina phoned. Her parents had bailed out her uncle, and they were going to stay with him for a few days. Except for testifying at his trial, there wasn't much more that they could do.

"We'll be happy to testify also," Stephanie said. "We'll be going home soon, but Leadville is only about a half hour from where we live."

Tina told Stephanie that she would make sure that her uncle's attorney had their name and number and thanked her for her support.

No one had much of an appetite at dinner that night, and there was very little conversation. After dinner the boys watched television while Stephanie tried to read one of her new books by Alice Chadwick. After several minutes of trying to get into her book, Stephanie joined her brothers in the family room.

"What if after we testify it still isn't enough to clear Arthur Duncan?" she asked.

"That's all you can do," Aunt Marybeth said, entering the room. "Now, how about having a bedtime snack?"

The teenagers quickly agreed and followed their aunt into the kitchen where they had milk and cookies.

The next day, the teenagers hung out at the house all morning. Tomorrow, their parents would be picking them up, and they had the mystery only half-solved.

"Let's go back to the arcade one more time before we have to leave," Steve suggested.

After several hours at the arcade, the teens headed back to their aunt's gallery.

"Who would like some ice cream?" their aunt said when she saw them looking so glum. "June, can you handle the gallery?" she asked, turning to her associate.

"Of course, I'd be happy to," June answered.

It wasn't far to the ice cream parlor, so the four of them walked down the block.

"I'm having a banana split with marshmallows and butterscotch on top," Stephanie said.

"Mmm, I think I'll have mine with chocolate on top," Steve said.

By the time they reached the ice cream parlor everyone knew what flavor they wanted. However, as they walked in the store their minds were no longer on what kind of ice cream to order. The men who had chased Tyler were at a table in the very back eating ice cream. Tyler nudged his brother and sister and motioned for them to act cool.

"We'll just watch them," he whispered.

After ordering the ice cream, they found a booth nearby where they had a clear view of the men. Aunt Marybeth, who was unaware of what was going on, was the first to speak.

"What's the matter with you kids, you were so talkative on the way over here?" she asked.

"We're just busy eating our ice cream," Steve said.

"Okay, if you say so," she answered. "So tell me about the clues again."

"I don't think that would be a good idea," Tyler whispered and then said even softer, "the wrong person might overhear."

"Oh," Aunt Marybeth smiled and then changed the subject. "Your parents will be back tomorrow from their trip. I hope they had a good time."

"They always have fun going places to do research for their assignments," Stephanie said.

Just as Stephanie had started to speak, they heard sirens coming up the road. All three teens rushed to the window to see a row of police cars coming up the main street.

"I wonder what's going on," Aunt Marybeth started to say, but the Thompson kids were already out the door of the ice cream shop and looking down the street in the direction of the sirens. A few minutes later, Stephanie and Steve walked back in to tell their aunt that Tyler went to get the truck and was going to pick them up in a few minutes.

"The sirens are headed in the direction of the warehouse," Steve explained.

"Yeah, we have to check it out," Stephanie added.

Knowing that the teenagers didn't want to miss the excitement, Aunt Marybeth said she would see them later. As the twins headed back out the door to meet Tyler, who had just pulled up in the truck, she yelled to them to be careful.

The Thompson kids followed the sound of sirens that brought them to the Bear Creek Bottling Company where they found a barrier of police cars. The traffic cop told them that they could not go any closer.

"We're working with Officer Johnston on this case," Steve said.

"Sorry, but I can't let anyone through," the officer said.

Tyler turned around but parked where he could watch for the police to leave.

"Why don't we try to get closer on foot?" he suggested.

The teens got out of the car as quietly as they could. Then, they found a tree and climbed up. It was a perfect view. They waited patiently for something to happen. Finally, the cops came out of the building with four men in handcuffs.

"They caught the thieves!" Stephanie exclaimed with a big grin across her face.

Tyler was giving Steve a high-five for their part in helping find the thieves, when he suddenly realized something. Even though they didn't have a very good view of the men, he knew they couldn't be the same men that had been chasing him.

"What about those men at the ice cream parlor?" Tyler asked, aloud. "If they are not the thieves then why were they chasing me?"

All of them knew that Tyler was right, so they rushed back to the ice cream parlor. At the shop, they found their aunt sitting at a table by herself with no one else in the restaurant.

"Aunt Marybeth, where did those men go that were sitting in the corner?"

"Do you mean those men that were at that back table over there," she asked pointing. "I would have introduced them to you but I didn't see them until after you kids had left."

"You know them?" Tyler asked puzzled.

"Yes, they came in my gallery one day, and we just started talking," Aunt Marybeth replied.

"What did you talk to them about?" Stephanie asked.

"Oh, just different things, art, antiques and stuff," she answered.

"Do you know where they went?" Steve asked.

"No, why all the questions, and did you find out what the sirens were for?" she asked.

"The police took four men out of the warehouse in handcuffs," Steve explained.

"It seems as if we were on the right track about the thieves hiding out there," Tyler added.

"Oh, thank God that is over with," Aunt Marybeth said as they left the ice cream parlor. "So what are you going to do the rest of the afternoon?"

"After we phone Tina and tell her the news, we don't have anything special planned," Stephanie said.

"You should go visit her since tomorrow will be your last day here," she said. "I have to go run some errands."

After the teenagers had said good-bye to their aunt, Stephanie spoke up.

"I wonder what all that was about?" she said.

"What do you mean?" Steve asked.

"Well, maybe it's just my imagination, but it seemed like Aunt Marybeth was trying to get rid of us," Stephanie answered.

"She probably has a lot on her mind with the robbery and all," Steve said.

The others agreed and nothing more was said about Aunt Marybeth as they walked down the street to find a payphone so that they could call Tina right away. They had only walked a few blocks from their aunt's gallery when Stephanie noticed an art gallery that had closed.

"Many people will be happy to find out that they caught those thieves," she said.

"Yeah, maybe some of them will be able to reopen their galleries," Tyler said.

"Maybe the word is already out," Stephanie said, pointing to the shop window. "It looks like those people are getting their gallery ready to reopen."

As the teenagers glanced in the window, they saw that she was right. Three men were inside painting the walls and ceiling.

"Wait a minute," Steve called. He looked in the window that Stephanie had pointed out. The others were already ahead of him and he motioned for them to come back. "I think you guys should take a closer look at this."

The others joined Steve to see that the three men inside were not just painters but the same men they had seen at the ice cream parlor!

❧

Chapter 10
Resolved Question

The teenagers only glanced in the window for a minute because they didn't want the men to also recognize them. What were they doing in a gallery shop that had just closed down? It appeared that they were getting the gallery ready to reopen. Could they possibly be thinking of selling the art they had stolen? Steve mentioned this idea, but the others disagreed.

"If they did steal art, I don't think they would have the nerve to try to resell it in the same area that they stole from," Tyler said.

The teenagers watched them through the windows until one of the men glanced toward them.

"We better go," Tyler said.

The Thompson kids decided to head right over to Tina's house to tell her the good news.

"That's great!" she said. "I have to phone my parents right away and tell them."

"The arrest should help put the case against your uncle in doubt," Steve said.

"It sure looks that way," Stephanie said.

"Would you like to catch a movie with us?" Tyler asked.

Tina quickly took Tyler up on his offer.

"I would love to get out of this house," she said.

Luckily, a new science fiction movie had just come out that they all wanted to see, so there wasn't any problem agreeing on a movie.

"Why don't you come and have dinner with us?" Stephanie said. "I know Aunt Marybeth won't mind."

"Are you sure?" Tina asked.

With Tyler and Steve both backing Stephanie up, they talked their friend into coming back to their aunt's house.

"I was wondering where you kids were," she said when they walked in the door. "Wash up for dinner. It's almost ready."

"Aunt Marybeth, I would like you to meet Tina Duncan," Stephanie introduced her friend.

"It's nice to meet you, and I am so happy to hear the good news for you and your family," Aunt Marybeth said.

"We are all relieved," Tina said, smiling.

"Is it okay if Tina has dinner with us?" Stephanie asked.

"Oh, of course," Aunt Marybeth said.

After dinner Tyler tried calling Officer Johnston again. He was excited to hear from him.

"Tyler, did you hear we caught the thieves?" he said.

"Yeah, we know, we saw you take them away," Tyler told the officer. "But something is wrong. They can't be the thieves."

"What do you mean?" he asked.

"The men you arrested are not the same men who chased me," Tyler said.

"Well, I don't know why those other men were chasing you, but we have the right guys, they have already admitted to the robberies," Officer Johnston said. "We even tricked them into admitting that they robbed the gallery in Leadville."

"The men that were arrested already admitted to the robberies, including the robbery in Leadville," Tyler said as he hung up the phone.

"Hurrah," Tina shouted.

"That's great news," Stephanie said.

"Officer Johnston has a call into the Leadville police department to clear up any doubt that Arthur Duncan is innocent," Tyler said.

"Thanks to you guys," Tina said smiling. "If you had not found the matchbook with the Bear Creek Bottling Company, we would still be looking for them."

"Tyler, why do you look so confused?" Aunt Marybeth asked.

"I still would like to know what those other men were up to," Tyler answered.

"Oh, enough already. The men that the police have arrested already admitted to stealing the art," Aunt Marybeth said.

Their aunt was right. It seemed like the teenagers had spent their whole trip trying to solve mysteries.

"Since tomorrow is our last day," Tyler said, "I think we will spend all day with you at the gallery."

"That would be great," their aunt said. "You can help me pack everything."

"What?" all three teenagers asked in unison.

Their aunt explained that she had decided to close down the gallery and open a bed and breakfast.

"I have been thinking about getting out of the retail business, and these robberies were the last straw," she said. "I've had my eye on this little bed and breakfast not too far from here. The owners want to retire, so they put it up for sale."

The teenagers agreed that it was a great idea as they listened over dessert to their aunt's plans.

Tyler, Steve, and Stephanie helped their aunt the next day, wrapping and packing up all her art. She was selling it all to a new shop that was opening down the street. June, who had worked with Aunt Marybeth many years, also helped them.

"I'm going to miss you, June," she said.

"Don't worry about me. It's time I retire, and I'll be around. You can't get rid of me that easily," June said.

After loading several boxes in the car, their aunt drove down to the shop. It was only a few blocks away so the teenagers walked since the car was so packed. They looked for the name of the store that Aunt Marybeth had told them about, 'Art and More.'

"Here it is," Stephanie said, as she looked through the window and then she gasped.

"What's wrong?" her older brother rushed to her.

"It's the shop that we walked by yesterday where the men were painting inside and look! The same men are inside!" she said.

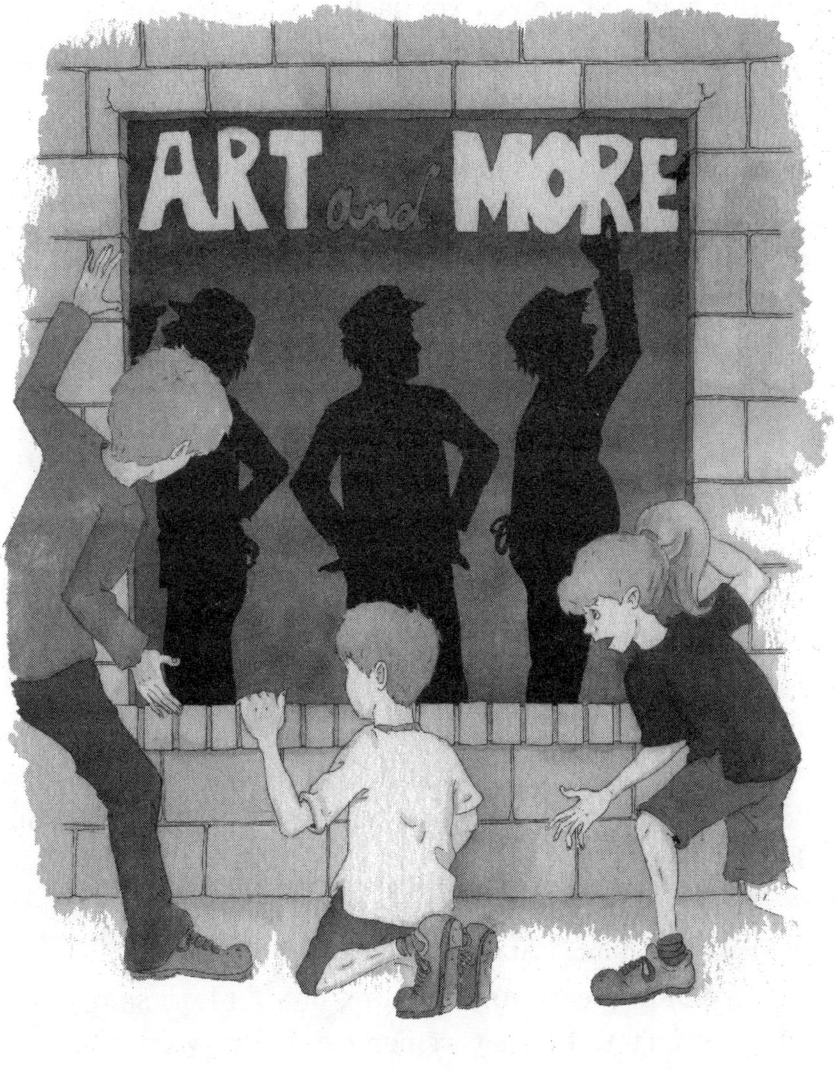
ART and MORE

As the teenagers walked in, their aunt smiled and said. "Come on in, I'd like you to meet Michael, Mark, and Kevin. They are the ones buying most of my art."

"Hi," the man named Michael said. "We saw you at the ice cream parlor, but you rushed out and then we had to leave before you got back."

"Aunt Marybeth, you said that you just talked to them in general about art and stuff," Stephanie said.

"I know, I wanted it to be a surprise," she said.

"These are the men that were chasing me!" Tyler said.

"Sorry about that, we thought you were an art thief," the man named Mark said.

"Yeah, we were trying to corner the market on Bruce Duncan art, but the art has been hard to find and we saw you eavesdropping," Michael said.

"We thought you wanted to find Bruce Duncan art to steal!" Stephanie said.

"What about flying to New York?" Tyler asked the man that he knew now as Kevin.

"Yes, I flew to New York to get money to open this store, that's where I'm from, but how did you know about that?" Kevin asked.

"We saw you at the airport," Aunt Marybeth said.

It was all starting to make sense to the Thompson kids, except one thing.

"What about the warning note that you left on Aunt Marybeth's door?" Stephanie asked.

"We didn't leave any warning note," Mark said.

It wasn't until they remembered the warning note

that they realized that the men whom Tyler was following in the blue pickup truck were the same men arrested.
They must have been the ones to leave the warning note;
after all, they had noticed that they were being followed.

"No wonder the voices on the tape didn't match
yours," Tyler said.

"Sorry to have misled you kids, but we really meant
no harm," Michael said.

The Thompson kids felt bad and apologized to the
men. They were all laughing over the confusion when
their parents walked in the door.

"Hey, what's so funny?" their dad said.

"It's a long story, Dad," Tyler said as he gave him a hug.

"How did you find us, Jack?" Aunt Marybeth asked.

"Oh, a June bug told us," he answered.

"Ha, ha, very funny, Dad," Steve said.

"The June bug said you are finished with the art
business," Carol said.

"That's a long story, too," Aunt Marybeth said. "How
about we fill you in at dinner?"

That night at dinner, there was nothing except
excitement as each of them took their turn telling the
sequence of events that had taken place. When they
were done telling about catching the art thieves, their
dad asked if they had done anything for fun.

"Oh, sure. We spent plenty of time at the arcade, not
to mention the movies and the mall," Stephanie said.

"You went to the mall?" her mother teased.

"We also went on our camping trip with all kinds of camping gear from Aunt Marybeth," Steve said.

"Oh, yeah, we didn't tell you about the attic," Stephanie said, and went on to tell her parents about everything they had found in the attic. "We even found an old Colorado map."

The Thompson kids didn't know it yet but that map would come in handy for their next mystery, <u>Marked Evidence</u>.

"I was about to tell you kids about the Palace of Governors in Santa Fe. After hearing everything that you kids have been doing, I doubt the historical exhibit would be as interesting," Carol Thompson said.

"I'm always ready to hear about historical exhibits," Tyler, whose favorite subject is history, said.

"We can tell you kids about our trip during the drive home," Jack Thompson said, smiling. "I'm sure you'll also be interested in the Escalera Famos."

"You visited a famous staircase?" Tyler, who had studied Spanish, asked. "Why is it famous?"

"The Loretto Chapel was built in 1873 as a home to the Sisters of Our Lady of Light, who started a school for women in Santa Fe. In the Chapel, the staircase has 360-degree turns. It has become famous because there is no visible support in the center of the staircase. There is a legend that says the carpenter who built the staircase appeared out of nowhere and disappeared in the same manner."

"That sounds neat, all right. Send me copies of the articles you write about it," Aunt Marybeth commented as she said good-bye to her brother and his family. "We've had so much excitement around here it will be strange getting back to normal."

"Yeah, we will miss you, but it will be nice to get home. I can't wait to see Lucky and Sammy," Stephanie said, referring to their cat and dog.

"Good old Sammy," Steve commented. "I can't wait to play fetch with her."

"Well, I know one thing," Jack Thompson said. "The next time Sammy runs off, I know where to find some good detectives."

"Now just where might that be, Jack?" Carol Thompson teased.

~

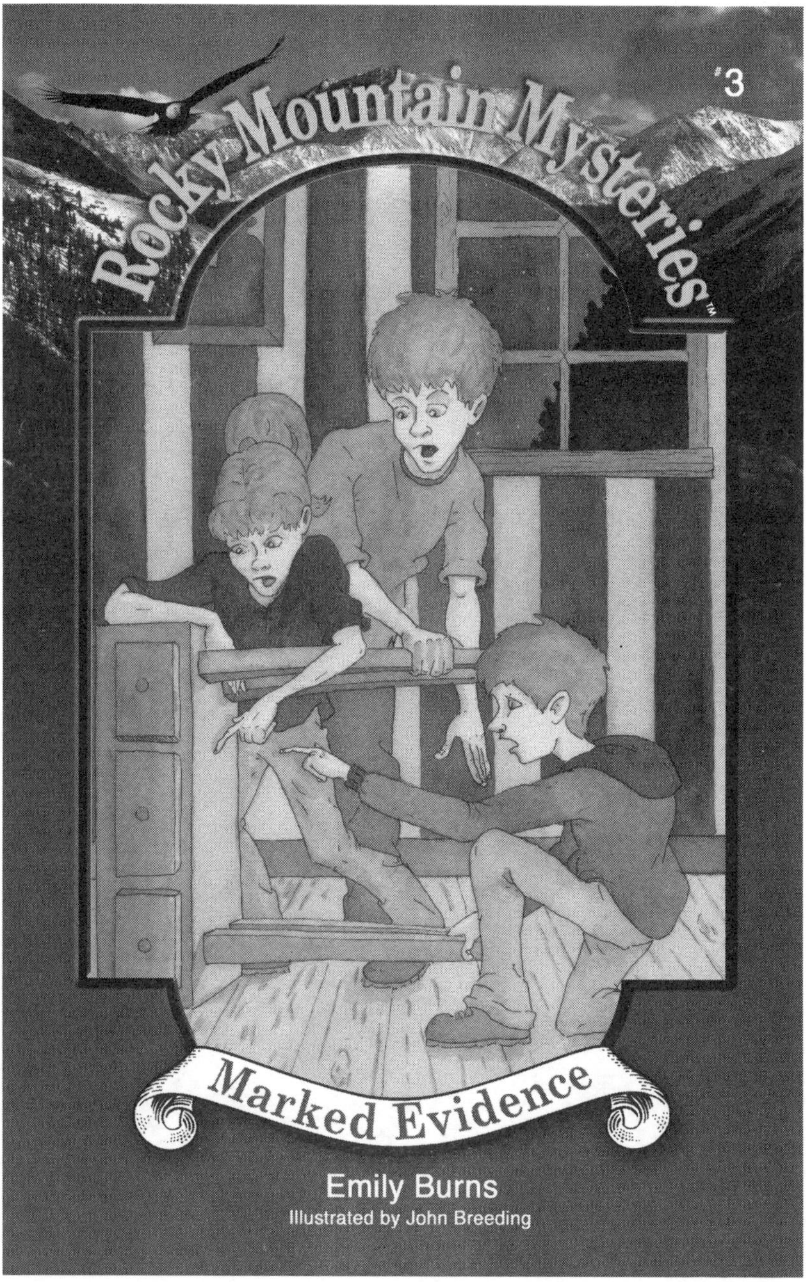
#3
Rocky Mountain Mysteries™
Marked Evidence
Emily Burns
Illustrated by John Breeding

Read a section of our next book, <u>Marked Evidence</u>

As they started looking at the antiques, the teenagers immediately sensed that something was wrong.

"What's the matter?" Tyler asked.

"Something isn't right about this table," Aunt Michele said.

"You're right," Bobbie said. "It's only a reproduction."

"What do you mean?" Stephanie asked.

"Sometimes reproductions are not easy to spot but this table is definitely not authentic," Bobbie answered.

"Does that mean we brought back furniture that isn't worth what we paid?" brown-haired Tyler asked Bobbie.

"I'm afraid so," she answered with a sigh.

"We were swindled!" Tyler exclaimed.

Rocky Mountain Mysteries™

#1

Mystery on Rampart Hill

Emily Burns
Illustrated by John Breeding

Did you miss our first book, <u>Mystery on Rampart Hill</u>?
Read a section of it to see what you missed.

From the outside the house looked huge. It was a two-story blue colonial that badly needed painting. The large wrap-around porch had round columns in the corners and on either side of the front stairs leading up to the porch. There were five large windows in the front and one big picture window. The teenagers had often thought about going into the abandoned house, but they had never ventured inside.

"Should we try the door?" Steve asked his brother.

But before Tyler could even answer, they heard a loud angry roar come from inside the house.

Check it out!

Our website address is:
RockyMountainMysteries.com

- Be the first to know what titles in the series are coming next.

- Find out where you can meet the author and get a book signed.

- Get to know more about the characters in the books.

- Learn historical facts about the Rocky Mountain region.

- Check out our fun stuff link. It's loaded with puzzles and trivia.

- Link to other cool websites.

- Plus, special chat times will be set up to talk with the author!

- And, keep checking back as we will be adding to and updating our website often!

A Brief History
of Manitou Springs

The name "Manitou" is an Indian word for "Great Spirit." They believed that the spirit gave them the many mineral springs in the area as a gift, and that the bubbling waters were sacred. The natural springs were considered to have healing power. The small Victorian town was developed around this theory as people came from miles around with prescriptions from doctors to drink the water. In particular, many patients with tuberculosis came seeking a cure for their illness.

The silver boom west of Manitou Springs brought traffic through the town. The Denver & Rio Grande Railroad was built in 1880 and dedicated by Presidents McKinley, Roosevelt, and Grant. But by the 1930's, the town's economy slowed. The natural spring water was no longer thought to be effective medical treatment and was replaced with vitamins and drugs.

When the automobile was invented, Manitou Springs turned into a tourist town. The main street was lined with curio shops and had an outdoor arcade area. There were also many artists in the area creating an art community. Today, the town hasn't changed much. It is still a popular tourist spot with shops, art galleries, bed and breakfasts, and yes, even the arcade is still there. It is one of the few penny arcades still left in the country.

Most of the mineral springs in the area have been restored, thanks to the Mineral Springs Foundation organized in 1987. Walking tours of the fountains, called Springsabouts, is encouraged along with drinking the water from the springs.

Autobiography of Emily Burns

Emily Burns was only four years old the first time she saw the Rocky Mountains and fell in love with them. Growing up in Ohio, she dreamed that someday she would make her home in the mountains, and as she grew up, she realized another passion: writing. Even as a young child, she could often be found in some hidden corner writing or reading.

Having spent a lot of time with children, including work as a nanny, Emily has come to realize that writing for children is an area that comes naturally for her. In particular, she excels in writing mysteries for juveniles, which is still her favorite reading material even as an adult.

Today, she resides in Aurora, Colorado, just east of the mountains, with her daughter and husband.

Artist Bio

John Breeding is a talented young artist currently studying fine arts at his high school in Colorado. His artwork has appeared in many art shows, and he has received the Outstanding Young Authors and Illustrators Award. His plans for the future include college and a career in art.

Give the Gift of
Rocky Mountain Mysteries™
to your children, relatives, friends, or anyone with kids 8-12 years old
Check Your Local Bookstore or Order Here

☐ *Mystery on Rampart Hill* _____ x $4.95 = _____

☐ *Manitou Art Caper* _____ x $4.95 = _____

☐ *Marked Evidence* _____ x $4.95 = _____
    Available March 2003

Add $2.00 shipping for one book
plus $1.00 for each additional book = _____

CO Residents add
.18¢ sales tax per book = _____

Total Enclosed = _____
U.S. Funds Only
Please allow up to six (6) weeks for delivery

Name _____

Address _____

City _____ State _____ Zip _____

Phone _____

Email Address _____

Parents:
Fill out to pay by Credit Card or Order online at
www.RockyMountainMysteries.com

Please circle one   MasterCard   VISA

CC Number _____ Exp Date _____

Authorized Name _____

Signature _____

Make Checks or Money Orders payable and mail to:
Covered Wagon Publishing, LLC
P.O. Box 473038
Aurora, CO 80047
(303) 751-0992 Fax (303) 632-6794

Give the Gift of

Rocky Mountain Mysteries™

to your children, relatives, friends, or anyone with kids 8-12 years old

Check Your Local Bookstore or Order Here

☐ *Mystery on Rampart Hill* _____ x $4.95 = _____

☐ *Manitou Art Caper* _____ x $4.95 = _____

☐ *Marked Evidence* _____ x $4.95 = _____
Available March 2003

Add $2.00 shipping for one book
plus $1.00 for each additional book = _____

CO Residents add
.18¢ sales tax per book = _____

Total Enclosed = _____
U.S. Funds Only
Please allow up to six (6) weeks for delivery

Name _____

Address _____

City _____ State _____ Zip _____

Phone _____

Email Address _____

Parents:
Fill out to pay by Credit Card or Order online at
www.RockyMountainMysteries.com

Please circle one MasterCard VISA

CC Number _____ Exp Date _____

Authorized Name _____

Signature _____

Make Checks or Money Orders payable and mail to:
Covered Wagon Publishing, LLC
P.O. Box 473038
Aurora, CO 80047
(303) 751-0992 Fax (303) 632-6794